T0369486

IMPERIUM
DIAMONDS

Caught Up

Xin•Xin

iUniverse, Inc.
Bloomington

Caught Up

iUniverse books may be ordered through booksellers or by contacting:

iUniverse
1663 Liberty Drive
Bloomington, IN 47403
www.iuniverse.com
1-800-Authors (1-800-288-4677)

ISBN: 978-1-4759-1640-9 (sc)
ISBN: 978-1-4759-1641-6 (ebk)

Library of Congress Control Number: 2012907389

Printed in the United States of America

iUniverse rev. date: 10/05/2012

Acknowledgements

I would like to give thanks to the Divine God and my Ancestors for all their contributions to my life. Thank God for sending me the best Granddaddy ever L. Henry Baker. I wish you were here right now to teach me how to play the guitar and listen to me read my first book to you. I will never forget to mention a Special Memory of Mrs. Judy Candace for encouraging me to write and publish this book.

I would also like to give thanks to my family and friends. All Love to the Women in my life, to my Grannie Alberta M. Baker, my Mother Lue Cinda Baker-Olapade, my Godmother Darlene Harris and Miss Katie McGill. Special thanks to my cousins Natalie, NaKeitha, and Ny'Tarsha Williams for their assistance with typing and encouraging words, as I worked a full time job while attending the University of South Florida. "GO BULLS!!!" My dearest cousin Victoria Smith-Anderson. Thanks Nadine Wyatt. Thanks coming from the bottom of my heart to the College Hill Library and the Urban Libraries thanks for opening your doors, I would have never had the opportunity to be where I am or given the opportunity to attend and graduate college without you. Thanks to the Tampa Bay Urban League for giving me my first job at the age of 14. Thanks Mrs Brown and Mrs Gussy at the College Hill Pharmacy for giving me a job, teaching me the ethics of working and encouraging me to continue going to school. Last but not least thank you Michael McGrew of Legacy Publishing Group LLC for assisting and coaching me along the way, Dr. Asaru Alim Nu Tu'pak El-Bey for assisting me with the final touches and encouraging words. Khadirah Ma'at T'pak El-Bey thank you for igniting my fire lol . . . CHECK!!!

Chapter 1

Caught Up In the Midst

> "You would have never known of a rich black family in Tampa unless you were in the inner circle. For the most part, circles are at times easy to disguise and hard to penetrate. Regardless of what social class a person is in, we all face our own struggles."
>
> Xin•Xin

March 6, 2009

Sweat had already started breaking at Ron's brow as he exited the doors of Exciting Idlewild Baptist Church. Church services were over at 11AM. Right in the middle of the Spring Equinox, it seemed as if he were in the middle of another hot Florida summer. There is no other heat like Florida's humid air, so much pollen flying around, it could make you almost have an asthma attack.

The family was meeting over at Grandma's house after church, which was the normal Sunday ritual. The one thing about family is building relationships. What better way to do that then by breaking bread, a dance off, sharing drinks, playing Taboo, throwing your feet up and watching a good movie or chillin not stressing about a thing.

Ron's simmering in his Sunday's spiritual cheer, decided to skip singles class and head right over to some good ole soul cooking brewed right out of the love of his one and only Grandma's heart. Driving on the interstate headed to I-4 Ron flipped on "Never Too Much" from the Luther Vandross' Greatest Hits just enjoying this positive vibe he received from church this morning. It was a beautiful Sunday; the thought of missing Grandma's cooking for the beach was highly unlikely for today. His stomach was just yearning for something to hit that spot. He had to eat something that he knew a drive-thru restaurant couldn't take care of. His hunger pangs made the trip to Thonotosassa feel like long extended journey.

The thought of speeding up crossed his mind, but was immediately cancelled when he heard the familiar chirps coming from his police radar. After almost an $175 increase in tickets and license renewals since Florida had all these budget cuts, Ron was not simply going down for putting any extra dollar into the city or government that had already taxed his pockets for the year. It was a construction area . . . looks like the city is taking forever to prepare for the Olympics, that's if they even meet the qualifications and requirements. Oh well God is still working on my patience. Seems like he's putting as many things as he can in front of me to make me slow down lately; and I'll just be . . . here's another tourist from Rhode Island jumping in front of me and slowing down, in the fast lane . . . Shhhh . . . .

One of these day's I'm going to come home to Grandma's and surprise her with my fiancée. I know they are going to be taken aback. It has been some years of dating and it seems like I can't seem to make a connection with a good woman. I would often think to myself . . . maybe, my Honey list is too long? You know women have their Honeydew list for their men and I have my Honey list for what I want in a good woman. Women who have locked down men, and I'm not talking about 6 months, I'm talking years, those women brought something to the table much more powerful than good sex.

To be honest and frank, I'm just moving around doing too much at this point to focus in on a relationship. My patience is short with DRAMA and stupidity. My type of woman though is dark, thick, has her mind right and her shit together. Right about now, every woman who even thinks of dating me is going on a live and exclusive interview at Starbucks. How this economy is going. I'm sticking close to all my money. I absolutely refuse to spend another dime on a chicken head or gold digger. I need the type of woman that I can spend all day talking to; who I can build an abundant life with. It is imperative that we have a connection deeper than the physical attraction or simply Pussy? And by Pussy, I mean the woman's only value to that man is to satisfy his physical needs. Her job is to make him cum. Pussy isn't just the hoe; the slut or the jump off, it's also the girlfriend who men have no intention of marrying or keeping around past a year. Nevertheless, the day of the Sugar Daddy is over, I am a prime time financial analyst. My new motto, "if she doesn't make dollars, she doesn't make sense." Because women can either make you or break you. I want someone who can stand right by my side and support me physically, mentally, and spiritually. In my mind there's no need for a divorce when everything is lined up at the door. We both would have an overstanding of what we each need from each other.

I'm just sick and tired of some of these lame as motherfuckers in Tampa fucking over some of these women. I better not find one fucking over any of my sisters. They are my heart and there's too much STDs and AIDS being spread around these days and as "man-made" and as "oxymoron" AIDS is; I wouldn't want to have to take them, nor myself to Dr. Sebi. The thought of one of my family members getting it might make me lose my mind. I will support them but the motherfucker who fucked them over I have no love for.

A woozy feeling came over me as I got caught up in my emotions and the sun's heat made a little moisture form to my body. Thonotosassa Exit—10 minutes away. I turned to 98.7 to listen to some smooth jazz to ease my nerves, because I didn't know what to expect.

Well I was the first to arrive, since church services at Exciting Idelwild Baptist Church let out fairly early than most of those sanctified churches. I remember visiting a COGIC church with my mother off of 22nd Avenue one Sunday. They let you out of morning services between 2pm to 3pm, which tripped me out, how they expected you back into service at 6:30pm to 7:30pm. It's just so funny how some of those sanctified people get so caught up in the spirit that they faint, form at the mouth, supposedly speak in tongues and waddle on the ground. It looks more like demonic possession to me. Anyway, my synopsis is people know that it's hot in Florida for one thing. Second thing it's after 2 or 3pm it's time to eat, the body is exhausted from all that running around the church like they are in a 5K triathlon and that's the only exercise some may get through the week.

I see a few cars parked outside as I pulled into this extended driveway. Yeah the infamous quadruple was there, consisting of Grandma, Great Aunty Louise, Aunty Geraldine and Aunty Joyce. Now Grandma was the glue that kept the family together. Years ago she had a hair salon and owned a dry cleaner down on 7th Avenue. Her hair was always done and when you talk about fashion, Grandma always had the best. She was very down to earth. She never had her nose too far in the sky and she would always be looking for opportunities of keeping colored folk working. She would always maintain her house and have dinner served at 6pm. She also made sure everyone had their baths and clothes ready so that everyone would be to bed by 8pm and ready for the following day. "You have to pay the cost to be the boss," she would always say. My grandparents were always family oriented so all the family from my father's side and my mother's side would be together on Sundays. They wanted to make sure that we knew who our kin-folk were.

Grandma loved elaborate things and having a pink and white mansion with her English Garden tucked away in the woods suited her well. You can't tell me if she didn't love her sorority colors. AKA FOREVER, "Ssssskiiiiwweeeee!!!" Now, for a woman to have taste at her age is not rare. My Grand Daddy and Grandma always hosted big parties at the house every summer. You would see some of the big wigs in town all gathered around to feast at this house. You're talking about live entertainment. Grandpa was apart of this local quartet group and all the members would show up and show out. You are talking about a blues festival in our own back yard.

Grandpa was the town's B.B. King. He could make that Bass guitar talk, which accompanied his deep silky voice. His dark skin, wavy hair, and tall stature distinguished him from the rest of the group, but they were together. They would ask, "You can make it if you leave . . . what's holding you up?" Grandpa simply told them, "I have a wife and child at home." It didn't matter about how light or dark skinned you were in there times because they all knew that in the end of the day all that they had were each other.

Grandpa is what you can call a free spirit. He was known throughout town for being a very charismatic comedian. No matter where he would go people were just be drawn to laugh and listen to him. He was a reporter for the Florida Sentinel and the Tampa Tribune. "If you work hard you have to play hard son," he would always say. He sung with the Quartet Group on Friday Night's at the Fox, Saturday he played baseball in Belmont Heights and to balance him off he would spend Sundays with family.

Tampa is known for its down home blues and the feel of Black love just filled the town. Everywhere you went people always greeted each other even if you didn't know them. Each little section of town had its own culture and people would come together sharing the latest gossip and food. All around some good old music, a few games of backgammon, cards, chess, dominoes and micanobe, Yeah those were the times. There was Great Uncle Al always on the barbeque and in the kitchen showing his new female friend how a man is supposed to cook in the kitchen with so many women flocking around him. It was like Uncle Al had a different friend each summer. He ran a chain of restaurants and for the summer he would come and stay with Grandma and reminisce on the days they grew up together.

Hum, I just wonder if I should go in now or wait for 30 minutes. They may be in the house praying and catching the Holy Spirit. And I know for a fact I'm not trying to get caught up. I will be the 1st one to raise my finger and head straight for the exit

Letting down my window I didn't hear anything, but I smelled the savor of fried chicken and smoking collard greens in the air. I think it's safe to go in. Let me make sure that I have my grown man on because these ladies will pick every inch of dignity out of you if you let them. The thing is everyone is wondering when I'm going to finally settle down and have a family. Knowing that they just want something else or should I say "fresh news" to talk or gossip about. Hummmm

RING RING RING

"Who is it?" a voice blurted out as the sound of feet paced to the door.

"Ron," I said.

"Hey baby, come on in!" Aunty Joyce, my Mom's older sister, said as she greeted me with a hug and kiss as I walked in. Aunty Joyce wearing her Red and Black Delta shirt and jeans it's another Sorority Show Off Sunday. We'll see who wins. Last time it had gotten so heated that Grandma simply had enough and kicked everyone out of the house, I was no exception to the rule. After that one incident you would think that that was enough. Here we are again, I want to make sure I get my stomach filled and have a paper plate wrapped in foil paper for my lunch on tomorrow.

Walking through the house was almost as if you were walking through an African and Roman collector's gallery. There were pictures of the family mixed in with personal portraits with some famous people that Grandpa and Grandma had known. Grandma usually would have her drapes open from time to time to see who was coming and going to her house. Certain parts of the house had white Victorian furniture with hints of gold which always kept this fresh look. While on other parts of the house she liked to keep up with the Joneses with modern designed furniture. On this particular day she was in the kitchen cooking up a storm.

"Who is that?" Grandma's loud raspy voice sounded like an alarm coming from the living room. After the heart ache of losing Grandpa over prostate cancer Grandma has put on 50 pounds. It looked as though she didn't give a care in the world of her health. Doctors had told her that her body was taking it hard with her rheumatoid arthritis and sudden weight gain that she should take it easy because she had developed diabetes. In 83 years of living she really didn't care.

"It's me Granny,"

"Is that my Ron-Ron?"

"The one and only, I'm the real McCoy Momma."

Grandma smiling with open arms, "That's who I thought it was."

"What you have cooking in here???" The one thing is to make Grandma mad, but I know that her cooking always suited my belly and soul quite well. After a certain age we are all set in our ways and canned yams, fried pork chops, collard greens cooked with hog jaws, and fried chicken was not going to change from this country woman's taste pallet.

As I walked around the corner I was like **OH DAMN**. If they ain't praying they gossiping and I'm fresh meat. "Hey Aunty Louise, Geraldine how are ya'll doing?" I said as I went straight for Grandma and went around the room to give my hugs and kisses.

"Fine, just fine baby," Aunty Geraldine said, my mother's younger sister, who always knew how to get on my nerves.

"Alright, that's my boy," Aunty Louise said, my father's twin sister, who always had my back. She was my shield of protection. I couldn't do anything wrong in her eyes.

"Sit on down son, you have to gone and tell us where you been hiding, and what's going on in your life." Grandma said.

"Just taking life as it comes Grandma. I just came back from Atlanta off of vacation and looking at my other company there. I 'm considering opening another branch in Ohio," I said as I made sure I sat down trying to avoid any of grandma's accessories. One break can land you on Grandma's D-list.

"Uhhhh—huuuhhhh, I hear it's a lot of gay men up there. You ain't tipping around, are you?" Grandma asked.

"Here we go, no Grandma I don't get down like that. Now you know . . . . ," I said.

"Well I know it's a lot of DL men now a days, I saw Oprah," Aunty Joyce said as she just added gas to the fire.

DAMN

"Well, I know what the Bible says about all that, but this day and age these young people choose whatever they want to, they like it, I love it. I ain't got nothing to do in the final thoughts of what God has to say about it all, because baby surely I don't have neither heaven nor hell to put no one in. And if we can be real about it, God said that he does not judge. It's your own consciousness. A man is a law unto himself and no one else," Aunty Louise said as she took a quick wink at me to show me she's getting them off me.

"Ain't your son gay Joyce, I seen him at the movies one day kissing on a man?" Aunty Geraldine said.

Rising out of the chair to defend her son's lifestyle, "Who told you that; you know you're getting a little too old to see Geraldine. Besides, if he is, that's his God damn business. At least my son ain't gone to jail, have 5 different baby mommas and strung out on Meth. My baby graduated from Hampton College, running his own law firm and other businesses, have 7 houses, paid for my mansion, taking care of my bills and still giving me money. How do you like the way my cookies crumble?" Oh and the reason why I waited to tell you about Aunty Geraldine, she is my mom's sister child who is seven years older than her. They say she is her spitting image and the apple just didn't fall to far from the tree. Pick a nerve of Aunty Geraldine you best be ready to back whatever you have up. "I don't curse only God curses, I just use profane language," is her motto.

OHHHH SNAPPP

"Ummmm not in my house," Grandma said.

After that you could hear the pots steaming in the kitchen.

"Well Grandma, the women that I've been meeting these days have not been what you told me to catch. It's like you never know who you're getting these days. One minute I'm in love and the next minute she trying to find where all my money is coming from. Then in some cases women love DRAMA and you know I'm far from that. I had to cut the silence.

"Well you sure were head over heels for Katrina," Aunty Geraldine slipped in.

See what I'm saying, I can't even speak. "Well I'll tell you, that was my first encounter with love Aunty and I'll never try it again. Like I was saying, but then you have some that are over whelmed with personal issues and I'm not responsible for what some other man's dealing. Then you have others with low self-esteem and don't know how to speak up for themselves, I need someone to think."

"Well baby it's alright boy, you will find that special lady. She'll just come out of nowhere," Aunty Louise said as she leaned back to sip another cup of tea.

"Are you sure about that Aunty because this goose is not getting any younger," I said

Auntie Louise looking at me with a smirk on her face, "Yes boy, like I told you things don't always come easily. When she's into you, you will know. Actions speak louder than words."

"Alright Aunty Louise I'll take your words into consideration," I said agreeing quickly.

"Honey, if you are the man that you say you are she will compliment you," Grandma said.

"Make sure you take care of that woman and she will take care of you," Aunty Geraldine said putting her two cents in.

"Even swap even swindle." Aunty Joyce said with a quick squint.

"I tell you one thing you best watch out for Julian." Aunty Geraldine said.

UMM

"I'm just warning you to keep your ass covered."

"She ain't lying about that because that boy will talk to anything that has two legs and a face," said Aunty Joyce

"Well I know the women that Julian and I attract are polar opposites."

"Good Afternoon." Momma came through the side of the house in her church attire.

"Hey ol' girl," jumping up out of my seat to land a big kiss on my momma.

"That's a pretty suite Amber," Grandma said.

"Yes Ma, you haven't seen anything until you see this new dress I bought from Michael Kors Collection.

"Well alright," Grandma said.

"Church folk ain't holier than a penny with a hole in it," Aunty Louise said as she looked at Aunty Geraldine.

Shortly after, the entire family came in like a river and soon I would have to be headed to my house to get ready for the rest of the night.

Chapter 2

The Pleasant Hangover

When it comes to a town being known as Jook city . . . Tampa, Florida is where it's at. These hot summer day are like none other, it may be hot in Arizona or California . . . but there's nothing like the humid heat in Florida. Can I just say it again, it's hot. It's like perfect timing. Spring just ended and some of these women already taking layers of clothe off. What's the purpose of going to a strip club when practically all the women are wearing thin clothes giving all exclusive peep shows depending on which block you are on.

The entertainment sector usually pops off with Sundance Films in St Petersburg, 1st Friday's with A Degree or Better Productions the very famous Mahogany Lounge or Flirt, a KSMG, The Eye on Fashion or HAUTE 2012 by The Fashion Movement.

It was 11:30pm when I rolled up to the Cheesecake Factory Entrance at the International Mall with my custom made Infiniti QX. I had it custom painted with an Aqua-Green paint with custom spinners made of Aqua-Green rims with a hint of black on the inside. No one had seen anything like this before because this Jenkins had connections. "You know why? No one had even seen the Infiniti QX, because it was to debut out in 2007. It was clean and right . . . and you know why. It's because the damn thang had a watery pearl finish to it. So when you walked up on it, it looked as though it was washed.

I pulled up to the Valet, so that it would be parked right in front of the restaurants on the concrete, so when everyone showed up to party they would just be jaw dropping at the site of this truck. No, this was not the first time I pulled a stunt like this . . . so I stepped out of my truck with my chocolate shirt which matched my cream pinstripe and brown slacks from the Steve Harvey Collection. I quickly grabbed my matching coat with a brown handkerchief popping out of my top pocket to set it off. I was laced with the Stacey Adams, yes, the gators which were brown had me looking like I had stepped right out of an Essence Magazine onto the red carpet.

The Flirt Event accommodated the finest eligible bachelors and bachelorettes in the Tampa Bay Area. There was a crowd already there and people that were sitting outside on the patio tables were just gazing wondering who this man was walking down the side walk. I had a nice, graceful pimp walk, looking like a Denzel Washington replica, as I graced the presence of my friends. It was like I was walking on water. My walk was so natural and clean because my legs had that bow legged touch on it like Denzel. I was just smooth.

"Look at you, player . . . . OhhhhOhhhOhhh he done strolled up in here with the Denzel walk got the women hungry. Boy they about to eat you up tonight," said Kyle Jones one of my ace-boon-coons from Chamberlain High School.

"Yeah, like a chocolate Hershey's Kiss up in this mother fucker . . . ha haha melt in your mouth and not in your hands," said La'Gwuan Helt another homeboy from Armwood High School.

I shook my head with a big grin on my face and laughed, "Boy you crazy."

"Ohh ohhhhweeehhhhh yeah I see you, I see you." The other accomplice to the group came strolling behind me by the name of Kevin Anderson. "Boy that's a nice fit . . . what you wearing, because it's about to cut my neck . . . . you're looking like new money that just came on the scene."

"You know I had to buss out with the Steve Harvey you know my style, So Fresh, So Clean, so I can get in between . . . ." I stated as we stood posted on the patio near entrance of the Blue Martini.

Calm blue light's and a warm cool breeze made it so relaxing and tranquil just to go and sip a drink. The crowd was thick tonight so we just walked in the Blue and went to our reserved area and sat back to catch up. It had been three months that passed before we had chilled out with each other. “Man, Kyle I hear that market is about to blow for you in the real estate industry,” said Kevin.

“Word, word . . . flipping houses like hoe cakes around this bitch,” Kyle said.

“Yeah and I hear you about to tie the knot La’Gwuan,” I stated as I gestured tying a rope around my neck. Ha hahaha everyone laughed.

“Yeah you know it, it’s about that time. I have the money stacked in the bank. I have the house on one acre of land and you know I want to have some kids right now. I also had to make sure that my shorties have their college tuition paid for and a little extra cash on the side before they pop out the womb.” LaGwan said.

“So who’s the lucky lady?” I asked.

“What’s her name so I can check the black book for any of the special Anderson double barrel bang?” said Kevin.

“Shoot is she cute . . . do she have a sister, some friends?” Kyle asked anxiously.

“Yeah, her name is Shartel Patel and she brought all of them here tonight with her so without further a due it’s about that 1A.M. time to shake a ’lil’ tail feather out there on the floor,” said La’Gwuan.

La’Gwan shaking his head, “Yeah, I made sure Shartel and her friends were well taken care of with some Belvedere, Ciroc, Grey Goose, and Crystal at the table.”

“Shorty wanna ride with me . . .” lyrics from Young Buck aired across the club and it was La’Gwans’s fiancé, Shartel sitting with a group of her close friends at the table. Shartel’s eyes got big as she saw La’Gwan step on the scene a few feet away. She was not like any other East Indian girl, she loved her some brothers. Her parents did not approve of her dating black men. In their culture, said Blacks are called Sudras, for “Untouchables”. They wanted her to marry an East Indian guy of Indian descent that they had arranged before she was ten years old and believed in keeping the Hindi traditions. Shartel was just struck when she met La’Gwan strolling downtown on Franklin Street in the middle of lunch hour. Despite the odds that were against them it was a match made in Heaven. They had mad love for each other. Her other friends, Heather a

Caucasian journalist for the Tampa Tribune. Jameka, a local Black on Black Rhyme poet. Brandy a caramel complexion sister, who is an Executive Manager at J.P. Morgan and Chase. Olga, a Puerto Rican Tax Attorney. Yeah the brothers had a variety to choose from. Shartel jumped up from the table to meet her man.

"Smooches baby, thanks for the drinks," Shartel said as she laid a phat kiss on La'Gwan.

"No problem baby you know I have to look out for you." La'Gwan said with sparkles in his eyes.

Kevin bending over to Kyle, "This joker sprung . . . ha ha ha." Kyle busted out with laughter.

"Let's introduce our friends to each other." La'Gwan went around the circle of his friends who were some of Tampa's most prominent black bachelors.

Well you know the twelve to one man ratio of women to men in Tampa Bay. Shartel's friends were just a minor touch of the successfully diverse women in Tampa. "Well since we are on the scene of introducing, let me introduce you to my home girls. Oh and don't let me forget there are three dancing their hearts out on the dance floor," Shartel said as she shook her head.

Well you know if a woman is better looking or by some other aspect than another one, she just can't really stand the other but tends to put up with her ways, it's simply because she brings more beauty and charm to the group. These three Goddesses that took the dance floor was none other than Shantel, a wealthy realtor; Candace, a girl that was born with a silver spoon in her mouth and then there was LaKesha Lloyd aka Kesha, who had caught my eye. This girl was drop dead gorgeous you could see that she had some good genes. Her natural hair lay down past her shoulder blades. She looked like she stepped off one of Heather Jones fashion shows. She had on this baby blue dress that had a slanted purple zebra print aligned from top to bottom. She pulled the side of her dress up and was taking it half way to the floor. It was as if she was taking it with a nice, cute, and conservative stripper dance. But the thing is this girl took the floor. She was working it.

The creepy crawling feeling of somebody is watching you had crawled up the side of LaKesha's neck. She turned in the direction of the group and to her surprise all eyes were on her. But like something she had been yearning for had caught her eyes. Looking like Denzel she starred at Ron as if she was going to just eat him up.

"Umm Damn, girl you see those cats at the table? Don't look to quick," LaKesha said to the others on the floor.

"I think it's time we go and say hellooo," Candace said.

"Ummmhummm," Shantel said.

Shartel motioned for them to come over. Walking back through the crowd men was grabbing on them, but they had already known the agenda. They were to get with friends of La'Gwans'.

"Man, I got to have that," Ron said to himself.

"Hey, I have the one in the Red (Shantel), "Kevin said as he bent over to Ron. "That's cool I have the one in the baby blue, dog." I stated sternly.

"Men, these are my friends Shantel, Candace, and LaKesha." Shartel said.

"Hello," they all said simultaneously.

"My name is Ron." I just took the initiative to introduce myself to LaKesha with my hand stretched out.

She was like, "Oh my name is LaKesha, pleasure meeting you."

"You want to dance?"

Looking over to her friends, "Why sure."

As we made it through our first song together, I tried rubbing her in some places and her hands always guided me away. This was no easy young lady. Since I couldn't get her that way; maybe a nice drink may soften her up, "You want a drink?"

"Sure,"

The club suddenly went to a nice salsa mix of Hector Lavoe's Aguanile and the crowd went wild. I took LaKesha by the arm and escorted her to the bar. "What will you like to drink."

"Nuvo on the rocks."

Motioning for the bar tender, "Can I get a Nuvo on the rocks for the lady and a shot of Hennessy for me."

Within seconds this Latin lover comes to the bar and grabs LaKesha and takes her to the dance floor. As I waited for the bartender to get our drinks, I didn't want to cause no seen but I'll just let him have a nice dance with her then I go back and scoop her up. Though I'm getting my rhythm going to the Grand Jete Dance School and practicing salsa with Alftredo Estefes, by the winter I should be a true Salsero. It was like the colors coming from LaKesha dress just lit up the dance floor. As I went to go reclaim my woman, "Excuse me, but she's with me."

"Oh no hommie she's dancing with me."

"Nawwh essay this is mine."

"I'm no essay. I'm Boriqua all day son."

LaKesha jumps in, "Honey lets go get a drink."

Pushing me, "whatever carbon."

"Let's go," LaKesha grabbed me and motioned towards the guy.

Feeling LaKesha's tender hands touch around my waist I just calmed down, "Let's get out of here so we don't get into any drama."

"Oh you ain't man enough to handle this and you can take that Bitch with you."

I turned around and next thing I know my hand was around his neck. Security and my homebody's came in and escorted us out the door.

Chapter 3

3 Days Later

Just remembering those days when it was easy for a brother to lock in a relationship with a woman. All a brother needed to do was have a job, car, and enough money to take her out to McDonald's and a movie. I know what I'm getting ready to say will probably sound like some "Willie Lynch" shit, but now a day's it's the day of Miss Independent. A brother would need 2 to 3 jobs, a fancy car, and enough money to give a woman to go on a shopping spree every weekend. Let's not forget a Black woman has to have her hair and nails done. LaKesha looks more like a decent woman so I can just skip the Starbuck coffee shop date and take her out to the movies.

Humm with so many people in town that knows my entire family, I'll just take her out of town. She'll really get the wrong impression of me if all these women came from out of nowhere asking me how I'm doing. A nice dinner and movie at Cobb Theater does sound quite impressive. You know women love to be wined and dined especially if they don't have to front the bill. Let me call her now.

"Good Evening . . . How are things?"

"Great . . . just finishing up on a few things around the office, how are you?"

"I'm good. Just calling to check in on you, just wanted to take you out on a date this weekend, if you don't mind?"

Chuckling, "Hummm that sounds enticing . . . let me take a quick look at my schedule. I don't want to make a date with you and I already have plans and things . . . . Well this weekend looks a little clear for me what do you have in mind?"

"How about we both go out for a dinner and movie this weekend?"

"Sounds nice, I hear Tyler Perry has a new movie coming out this weekend?"

"Yeah, My Big Fat Family," here we go . . . I sure hope she doesn't try to give me any wedding bell signals, automatic strike on the first date.

"Okay, sounds like a plan . . . so what time where you thinking?"

"I would say I can pick you put around 6pm and we'll go from there."

"Okay, and where are we going exactly and which theater?"

"You don't have to worry, I will not bite, I was thinking more of Cobb Theater, since it's out of town and we can spend a little time getting to know each other."

"Yeah that's sounds like a deal." He just does not know I'm calling Shantel and Shartel and letting them know I where I'm at. After Lloyd beating the shit out of me and leaving me for dead. Don't have to tell me twice about leaving contacts for someone to find me. And I know I'm not going to be out all night because by the time we are supposed to be finished Shantel is going to give me a call.

Arriving at LaKesha's Condo down in Channelside. I made sure I called ahead of time to make sure my car does not get towed. Walking through the garage and taking the elevator to the 13th floor I made my way to the door hiding the bouquet of flowers. Ringing the doorbell, I hope things flow great tonight I made sure I didn't spray on to much of Sean Johns Unforgivable on because pollen is flying through the air. I don't want her to have any allergic reaction. I just want her to take it all in, basking in my ambience of a warm relaxed and gentleman ready to sweep her off her feet at the drop of a dime.

"Who is it?" this sweat silky voice questioned behind the door.

"It's me honey."

Taking her precious time to come to the door . . . building up this nervousness in me. "It's Ron." I wonder if she hears me? I know she heard me . . . she had 3 hours to prepare and still dragging.

"Oh okay," unlocking the door.

"How are you this evening?" presenting her with roses.

"Oh great, for me?" she astonishly asked.

"Why wouldn't it be for a special lady as you?" I asked . . . that should just melt the icing on the cake.

"OMG, Lily's, how did you know?" her eyes just opened and sparkled, smiling from t to t, she couldn't believe it.

"Well, it's my business to know what pleases you."

One eyebrow lifted and a smirk came to her face. "You can come in I have to grab my purse and accessories." She made sure she walked a little slowly ahead of me.

"You smell very good, is that Givenchy?"

"No"

"Polo Sport?"

"Close but Unforgivable."

"Unforgivable . . . hummmmm." her eyes looked me up and down.

"Hummm can I have a seat?" I gestured to the living room.

"It's just going to take me a sec . . . . well alright I'll be right back.

The earthly feel of her brown and chestnut bordered living room and auburn kitchen made it very warming. The apartment was actually cleaned. I am very impressed. The walls were adorned with family portraits and African Art. It took me back. I felt like I was in a daze looking around at things. In the kitchen area . . . she had two Chinese fighting swords on the walls complementing Chinese Calligraphy and a little book case that took the place of a China cabinet filled with Asian Books and Blue and White China. This woman had taste . . . not cluttered but the Fung Shui just let the energy flow through the room.

Coming out of her room, she had changed her clothes to complement my khaki shirt and brown jeans. A one shouldered brown dress with light brown stiletto heels. She changed her hair so that it would complement her ensemble. I most defiantly will not have to check her fashion sense.

"How do I look?" she asked slowly turning around just so that I got a peak at every angle and inch of her body.

"Absolutely stunning."

"You don't say?" this grimacing smile came over her face, "Well it's time for us to head on."

"There's nothing rushing us. So why not take this slow and easy."

"No, No now, I know we have a journey ahead of us so let's not be late."

"Have you ever been to Cobb Theater?"

"No, but I know that if we don't hurry up we are going to miss dinner and the movie."

"I can cook, and I know you have some DVD's around."

"Okay no, you can take me on a date."

"Okay no problem, just making a suggestion. Looks like you already know how to entertain." I slowly placed my hands at the small of her back.

She looked deep into my eyes and gasped for breath, "Yeah, dinner and a movie sounds great."

"After you."

"No, after you I do have to lock the door."

Laughing, "And you will be right."

LaKesha sure knew what she was talking about by the time we made it through all of those construction zones we barely made it for the last dinner. Thank God for GPS or we most definitely would have not made it.

What a surprise arriving in Wesley Chapel at the Cine Bistro there were so many Black couples having a great time mingling with their dates. I would have never suspected that Black people were out here. Most big companies called themselves downsizing and relocating to the Tampa Bay Area. So with the relocation has brought many northerners into the mix. Picking up tickets and escorting LaKesha through the doors . . . Moments later it was as if a Harlem Renaissance just hit the Bay Area, everyone was having a great time.

Arriving at our reserved table . . . pulling out the chair for LaKesha to sit in . . . . "Baby I have to go to the restroom."

"Okay I will be here when you return."

Looking at her as she made her way to the restroom, the waiter arrived asking, "What can I get you today?"

"I would like to order a bottle of wine. I would need an extra glass for my lady. The Duckhorn Merlot looks great."

"Okay,"

"You can give me minute I'll wait for my lady to return to order."

"I will be back in a minute with your bottle of wine and glasses . . . here are the menu for you two to order from. I will give you a second to look over them.

Arriving back at the table . . . Kissing me on the cheek, "Thank you for bringing me here it's really nice."

"Anytime honey."

"I ordered us some wine, what would you like to eat?"

"I think I want to try something out of the ordinary. New Year, New Things. I'll have the Pan Seared Atlantic Salmon."

"I won't compete with that."

"I'll have huuummmm . . ."

The waiter returned to the table, "Here's your wine, can I go ahead and take your orders."

"Yes she will be having Pan Seared Atlantic Salmon, I would like Steak House NY Strip"

Looking like children at Disney World we just looked around at the scenery and people watched, everything was just captivating . . . They say a few drinks don't tell any lies. Well LaKesha was on her second drink just before the food came. It was as if she transformed right before my eyes. I get a little close to her to make sure that she was secure then . . .

Placing her hand on my thigh felt so nice. I never had a woman show me so much affection on the first date. The majority of times I feel like I'm a talking to a time bomb one wrong move and it's like a man just set it off. At first it felt like I was walking on shells until she scooted her chair a bit close and placed her hand around my arm. Now, with all this attention I had to stay in my lane and play straight to the script because if I go down the wrong path this date could be over within a minute so . . .

Dinner was served and the aroma just was great. LaKesha's plate looked delicious almost as if I wanted to change plates . . . hmm honey that looks good.

"You want to try . . . She took her fork from her plate.

"I most definitely do . . ." Taking a bit of Salmon . . ."It is scrumptious . . . ummm umm honey that is great almost make me want to change what I ordered.

After the eating, the movie had was about to start LaKesha came close to me and we cuddled . . . The waiter came back removed our plates and it was my favorite Crunch and Bunch time and Wine . . . People just don't know that nuts and wine makes it potent. The lights dimmed and I snuck in a kiss on her lips.

Chapter 4

The beautiful sunny blue sky's cascading its pink and orange colors in the clouds marked the ending of a beautiful day. But the beginning of a spectacular night, traffic was jammed packed with the usual 9-5 workers all in sync to head home or some nearby happy hour. It's what you want to call the Friday's extra unwind of relief from a week worth of home or work related stress. Owning your own company gives you plenty of flexibility to enjoy your time with family and escape at any block of free time. Having a group of the best secretaries and office personnel that was dedicated to the job makes things easy. Like any company it's a network of interlinking relationships. Everyone depends on me to make strategic intelligent decisions while I rely heavily on each individual to implement and carry out the design. The company is always open for new ideas along with catering more jobs inside the company along with always have the option for promotion. One thing about business you always make sure you take care of your employees and they will always for the most part take care of you.

Having the company placed in the center of downtown Tampa it made it easy and feasible for our workers to take walks along Channelside, drop into John F Germany Library and catch a mat née at the Tampa Theater or symphony at the Tampa Performing Arts Center, or capture the essence of art at Tampa's Art Gallery. Tampa has expanded thanks to the governor Pam Ioria doing all upgrades on the city.

Making my last thoughts of the new ventures in Chase and Chinese companies, I made my way through the back streets and headed down Westshore. Having changed my clothes to my wind breaker and tee with my Rockawear athletic pants, I wanted to take time clearing my head from all these demands coming through my mind. I had parked at Ceviche and got a bite to eat and drink. Yes, all before 7pm so I don't get caught up with adding any extra pounds to my belly. I took to the streets and walked to Bay Walk. There were many people either sitting conversing, walking, rollerblading, or jogging.

Walking down the walk, Oh I almost forgot to call the crew because the minute I do something they always say that I'm so selfish that I didn't invite them.

"Hey La'Gwan, going to the rink on Sunday night just calling to see if you were up for it?"

Without a moment's hesitation and the snap of the pussy whip, "Let me see what Shartel wants to do."

I paused for a second to hold back from laughing, "Alright damn."

"Well, she's okay for coming out, she wanted to know if LaKesha and others coming?" He asked in his aggravation of asking all these long open ended questions.

"Yeah, she's coming so if you can all the crew and let everyone know."

"Do I look like Benson to you, I'm in the middle of eating and handling something you are going to have to handle that one this time."

"No problem, I understand, I'll just send a text."

"Alright handle your business man."

Before I could even get the words out to say good bye the phone had already hung up in my face, "DAMN!"

Slowly walking trying to coordinate and walk at the same time people just started rushing to the side of the sidewalk getting out of my way. Damn what the hell is going on these days people use to just give you a nod or quick hi and be on about their business, all of a sudden it's like I'm a criminal out here, like I'm just really about to do something. Oh it's just occurred to me with all this mass media of the degradation of Black people. All you read or see in the news is people either being robbed, jailed, or supplying people with drugs. The only way you come off free is as if you are in the NBA, a celebrity, or have been seen associating with people with money. And half hardly most of these foreigners sometimes get it twisted like we owe them something. Hell, Black people and natives were here long before Christopher even forged his lie into saying that he found Indus. It is amazing, how the people attempt to hide historical truths concerning our indigenous presence here in the Americas and how the Olmec is the oldest modern civilization in the Western hemisphere.

There are times that I would just leave out of town at a drop of a hat and head to Miami's Fashion Shows, up to FreakNik in Atlanta, Georgia or head further up to Black Bike week in Myrtle Beach, SC. Sometimes I feel like I just want to be in the wind like my Ancestor's and explore Kemet (Egypt), the Ama Zulu people of South Africa who speaks of their ancestors coming from Mars, the Nagas in Cambodia, Tibet, China and Japan, the Buddha Temples in Asia, go back and visit the Aboriginal people of Australia who say they came from the moon. Just getting out and being in contact with my African culture visiting down in Brazil, where the majority of enslaved of the Diaspora reside. I just need a woman that I can take around who does not have a chip on her shoulder. I do understand that there are many Black folk walking around angry and pissed off for reasons that they can't seem to comprehend. I need a woman with some form of consciousness, a woman that's here with me actually aware, where I can feel her loving energy. Too many sisters' are out of sight, hence out of mind.

"LaKesha how is your schedule for skating this Sunday?"

"Sounds alright with me Sweetie, but I have lost my entire concept of how to move on skates.

"Oh get out of here," I always believed that when you learn something you always will remember how things should be done. I couldn't help but to start cracking up on her.

"I'm serious since going off to college my entire perspective changed, there's nothing wrong with skating but everyone now is rollerblading."

"Honey its okay they have the old fashioned roller blades for you with that big donut sized brake in the front . . . Ha ha ha . . . it's alright your very special to me honey."

"There is nothing funny."

"Honey its okay once I get you skating on those skates you'll be in roller blades in just a few. I guarantee that."

"Are you sure Ron?" And I expect you to catch me before I fall not when or after I fall."

"Ha ha ha . . ."

"Ha ha hell . . . It's an absolute embarrassment to see my grown self on old roller skates in the middle of the skating rink one leg going one way and the other God knows where?

"Okay okay, I got you from what it sounds like you just lost your rhythm of things . . . Ha ha ha . . . probably even your coordination." I just had to put it out there because LaKesha has this competitive edge about her and she swears she's the best at everything that she does. I just have to bust her bubble on this one.

"All I know how to do is coordinate financial numbers, marketing and tradeshows. And you know we are both over thirty and anything we break or dislocate takes a pretty bit longer than usual to heal. That does not even necessarily mean that things will heal back into their proper place. And I'm definitely not trying to split a thing yet. I have yet to have children."

"Okay honey I'll take it nice and slow with you."

"Well I just have to go out and make a complete ass of myself, can I bring my crew?" LaKesha had asked frantically.

""Ha ha go ahead on, I can call my friends." I really wanted to spend time with her alone but this exception will be great. "Well I just have to let you know all my friends are not going along with the skating idea, so if your friends are coming they might want to brush up on their skills." I know I'm okay with saving one damsel in distress but a crew of women. I know the 1st thing they will want me to do rescue them then next comes the accusations of being to close or my hands slipped and touched something that I didn't have any business.

LaKesha got quite and cleared her voice as if we needed to go ahead and wrap this conversation up, "Well, you heard what I said, don't let me fall."

"Okay, Okay, so I'll see you on Sunday night at the rink off of Armenia, Thursday is crowded for you so we'll take it slow so you can actually learn how the art of skating is supposed to be done."

Blowing air over the phone, "Here we go," she loves to retaliate, "someone's head just blew up a little bit bigger."

"I'm just saying, I have to give it to you like it T I IS." I chuckled, trying to hold back my giggles, turning around at my desk.

"Got to go back to work will call you later hone."

"Talk at you later sweetie."

TGIF, it's like I have been waiting for this moment. LaKesha's getting off work and who want to come is more than welcome.

Sunday Night

There was to be expected spots of rain throughout the Bay Area for tonight. One thing I do know that Black folk do not come out in the rain for the simple fact of getting hit by lightning. As we all know Tampa means City of Thunder. Getting a Black woman's hair wet in the rain, ocean, or pool is just not cool especially if she just came from spending $50 to $1000 or more getting her hair done from whether the natural to it being weaved . . .depending on the sister, she either be calm and courteous and just ask her stylist who may or may not charge her to redo it or she will transform like a transformer into a pissed off angry at the world fighter and you might just want to get out her way. The other thing is people fear getting their new outfit messed up with the soak or plain out right getting sick. The best thing one could do is go somewhere and mind or tend to your business in a corner at home. When I was younger Grand Daddy use to always start a word of prayer and didn't matter who was down the street or what we were doing while we were at the house. The family would form a circle in the living room and Grand Daddy's long winded self would pray all the way until the rain stopped. So that meant you better hold it or run fast to the restroom and back because that nice prayer can turn into a sting from a switch.

I had intentionally brought my short hand umbrella with me just in case I have to escort LaKesha out the door. I also am going to make sure she's coming.

"Baby, I'm here are you on the way?"

"Yes, and I have taken my 3 shots of espresso and coffee what I call "RED EYE" so that I don't fall asleep so early or tire out to quickly."

"Alright, I'll be waiting. I'm standing on the inside so just park and come on in."

"Okay, that's the skating rink off Armenia right?" She questioned because she is known to forget things.

"Yes, sweetie."

"See you soon."

"Peace"

Running through the door looking all around LaKesha had my eyes glued to her every move. I could see right in between her legs and to my eye's delight her pussy was phat. Damn, but even phatter was that ass. It's like Mos Def said, "Ass so phat you can see it from the front!" She had on these skin tight jeans and yellow checkered farmer boy shirt with matching accessories.

"Umm, baby nice to see you."

"Ditto"

"You smell very good, what is that you are wearing?" I just had to reach around and get another hug from her.

"HummmHummm unlike you a woman never tells the name of her perfume." She said as she left my arms, my mind still in the clouds.

"Ohh, it's like that?"

"Ha ha you'll be okay honey . . . well it's called Flower Bomb," she said as she made her way to the counter.

"You have to fill out this card completely before you are allowed in."

"Say what they sure want to make sure they don't get sued and they have the Sherriff at the counter taking money."

"Yeah, you know how that goes too many Black folks at an establishment or in an area having too much fun folks get all scared." Gesturing.

Hitting me on the shoulder, "ha ha you need to quit, you know it's some real goons out here and most these men, not you baby, will just let them disrespect and mess up the entire get together. All you need is some liquor, weed, or another man hating on the other and it's on."

"Yeah, that's what they say. Melanin is like fire if a signal is sent out something is lying to explode or pop off. But I'm all for safety and keeping peace."

"Yeah our culture use to live in peace, no hard drugs or fighting amongst each other or lack of support like it is at this time, there were no jails either. Everyone stuck together and looked out for each other.

"Well, we know how that story ends, what you see are what you get the degeneration of a people. But let us just enjoy our evening together and start a new trend."

There was a line at the counter to pick up the skates. I could not wait to get LaKesha inside the rink. So many people were there. It was as if it were at a skate-off in Atlanta. LaKesha was astonished to see so many black people at the rink. There were no more questions of where's everyone at. Primarily the majority are either playing pool bowling sitting at home watching American Idol or Dancing with the Stars . . .

Arriving back at the house it was as if no one lived there and neighbors were at least half a mile away. I wanted to keep this house mainly to keep people out of my business. The houses that they recently built in New Tampa and in some subdivisions are so close that you can practically hand your neighbor ketchup or a glass of water out of the window.

Getting out of the truck and excorting her in the house I was like I hope Miss Gail's Cleaning Service, my personal cleaning lady, came around this week to clean and change my beddings and restock my food because last quarter I practically didn't have a chance to do a thing. Smelling the fresh scents of lavender and vanilla as we walked through, "Oh nice home." LaKesha said as we walked in.

"Thanks, let me give you a brief tour. Here is the den where I like to welcome people in. I just have Miss Gail to rearrange the house every few months because it makes you feel like you just came into a new dwelling. I love keeping the place filled with warm earth tone colors, I had had Albert to paint the outside and inside of the house.

"Wow he did a great job!"

Clearing my voice, "Yes he's so strategic he actually started painting homes and the age of 14 so the man has some skills that will blow your mind. I have been knowing him for years. Here's the living room you know a man's house is not complete without a flat screen, Al Pachino's picture on the wall, Playstation, P90X, and Xbox. Over here I added an island to the kitchen to open it out. When I first purchase this home and old couple decided to move further down south to Sarasota so they were trying to get rid of it, so mainly I've added on additions I usually have family or guest in all the time. This is like the best get away from the hustle and bustle life.

"Ohhhh" She said.

Guiding her further through the house, "Here is my office. If I need to have a meeting I just have it from this desk. I have a satellite system that is able to pick everything up."

"Wow impressive."

"There are three guest rooms on the first floor and upstairs we have the master bedroom suite. Would you like something to drink before we head up?"

Shaking her head, "Not really"

"Okay well here is where we'll commune for the rest of the night. I had my interior decorator Shari Hurst come on and make things happen, can't say you're a King if you don't have a castle." Going over to my refridgerator, "I have juice, water and drinks . . . Well . . . I'll just have me a shot of some Ciroc and grapefruit juice."

As I turned around turned around LaKesha was already in her bra and panties . . . Swallowing my drink, "Well, what a beautiful sight to see."

Slowly walking over to me, "So where are we going to start? or the Kitchen for a counter top special?"

Kissing her on her forehead and then her lips. Placing my hand at the small of her back and grabbing her ass, "UMMM, looks like this is going to be an interesting night."

Smiling and throwing her hair to the side, "Hummm that sound great, my mission for tonight."

Grabbing her leg feeling on her breast it was like grabbing on soft cantaloupe and going down to touch her pussy she was already wet.. GAME ON!!! I picked her up walked over the bed started hissing all over her body, "Baby can I taste?"

Looking at me with seduction written all in her eyes and biting her lip, "Why yes!!

See if you don't know how to eat pussy a good woman will just look at you crazy. Since she was already ready, I pushed her body up in the middle of the bed. Placing my lips on the lips of her clit and started rolling my tongue in a 360 degree rotation . . . she started to moan thrusting my tongue in and out until she made her first gasp of air. I came out, inserted my fingers in to hit her spot. She started shivering went back in for the kill with my lips in and out with my tongue this time I curved my fingers to tap on her g-spot

"Oh baby," she yelled.

Gave her a little tongue then I curved my two fingers tapped and buzzed on her spot and nectar just cam flowing all out. I went down and got my taste and it was the bomb shit . . . Feeling her body quivering. I turned her over and started giving her the Full Monte, "Umm this pussy still wet," so I started smacking her ass. She squeezed and put a vice grip on me, "Ummm that's what I'm talking about." I just kept on going in and hard. I pulled her leg to the side and then just started pumping even harder.

"Oh baby give it to me!"

"Umm you like that don't you?" I stated. Turned her over again on her back and crossed both of her legs and was in there.

She started grabbing her breast and licking her lips. "Give it to me Ron . . . ummm."

Next thing you know . . .

"I'm about to come again baby." Gasping for breath.

I had unwrapped her legs, pulled one over my back and she went out into another world. Yeah that's what I'm talking about done sifted her consciousness. She stayed out in space for a few minutes . . . Kissing her on the lips as she came back to.

Umm can't wait for my next episode.

Chapter 5

A ROMANTIC SWINDLE

Reaching LaKesha's house on Sunday, which was our day to be together. Sunday is considered family day being in a relationship with a good woman. Not just a good woman a fine, breasted, thick thighed, phat assed, long hair, dark woman is simply irresistible.

Just being in her presence is mesmerizing. She's hell during the day working at Verizon's corporate office but at night she changes into an entirely new person. It's like a turning off the light switch effect that happens when she crosses the door leaving work.

Reaching the rose shop, I had purchased a dozen roses and a bag of rose pedals.

"Must be a special someone?" The cashier said as she winked at me.

Just grinning, "Yes . . . what else would a woman like if she comes home to roses, nice music and a good man all unexpected? I will make a nice bubble bath and put roses all around it. You know because spreading potpourri around just wouldn't produce the same affect. "Butterummm I'll take that," reaching for my change.

"Well a diamond ring wouldn't hurt either!" She said with a sudden burst of laughter. This scary feeling crept up my back.

Arriving at LaKesha's house I noticed that she was already there.

Shit time for Plan B. Alright I'm going to go in the room; tie a scarf that I had purchased around her face, sit her in a room for 10 minutes, run back to my truck and get everything and go along with everything else as planned.

Tucking everything away, I made my way to the door.

Plan C

Catching up with this woman is extremely a challenge so I have decided that I would treat her to a romantic evening at the Good Luck Café this Sunday night. While strolling through International Plaza; I decided to pick up a nice diamond set to give Miss Lloyd. Being charming, romantic, and knowing how to treat a woman simply came easy. This is my pride and joy so I have to take care of her so she won't tip out on me with another man. She knows what she has at home.

"Baby, this is so nice of you to bring me here. You don't know how exhausted I am from this week," said LaKesha.

"Umm."

"I tell you if it wasn't one thing it was another."

"Alright baby for this moment let's just focus on the time we have together right now."

Looking into her eyes, she simply melted. The dinner was served and the night was young. Smooth Groove began playing music. After the second set, "Why don't you come back to my place tonight?"

"Umm"

"I have a nice Jacuzzi you can take a bath in and I have these nice techniques to massage your feet. I ain't trying to brag or anything but I did graduate from Erwin Technical Institute and I do have my massage therapy license so you don't have to be scared. You can enjoy the rest of the night in my arms."

"Ohhhh, that's right up my alley. You ain't said nothing but a word."

"So are you ready?"

"Well, I put in a special request to hear something; they know me so well down here."

The thing was that two working people, hardworking individuals, find it hard to find time for each other. This night right here was simply special. Driving down Kennedy Avenue and making a left at the University of Tampa the weather was beautiful.

Going across the bridge towards Davis Island and making our way to my tucked away mansion.

"Oh this is your place?" LaKesha asked.

"Why yeah, were you thinking I was headed to Brandon or something. Yeah this is far fetch from the hood baby."

"I wasn't saying that, but this is absolutely gorgeous."

"Yeah . . . ."

Chapter 6

Another Distinguished Gentleman

Wednesday 12PM at J Alexander's

I don't know what in the world baby girl got going on I just hope it ain't no surprise. I don't have time for no drama. I'm feeling a little uneasy since I came back from the doctor diagnosing me with Diabetes. Diabetes must have been some kind of genetic dysfunction or pancreatic malfunction because I know that I'm one of the healthiest men on earth. I heard that raw string beans, lots of cinnamon and exercise controls insulin levels, might have to head to Chucks or Whole Foods once I leave.

It was stressful even coming to this place. I had to take the Downtown East West to avoid the 12 o'clock traffic on the interstate. Jumping out the truck with my Jordan outfit and white t-shirt, women were breaking their necks trying to get just a slight acknowledgement from me. How about NO!!! I paid them no mind as I grabbed the door and gave this woman free entry into the building. You know I have to have my grown man on and show these women that there still is real gentleman that exists.

"Hello and thanks for visiting J Alexander's how may we help you Mr. Jenkins," the host said.

"Yes I'm here for a Miss Jenkins."

"Oh okay right this way."

Walking in the dimmed restaurant I see my baby girl and some cat by the window. Here we go with this shit.

"Hey Ron," Jumping from the table to greet me with a hug and a kiss.

"Hey baby girl. Who is this?" I said without hesitation.

"Sorry baby but my brother is quite blunt and straight to the point about things," Jaya said looking me in the eyes.

"Lloyd Hawkins, nice to meet you," he got out of the seat to shake my hands.

"Ron, what's up?"

"I already ordered your favorite, you want some spinach dip," Jaya said.

Umm trying to sweet talk me into something, must want something.

"Well, I brought you here to meet Lloyd. We have been together for 2 years . . . .

"Well, why don't you let the man speak for himself," I said, because I know Jaya, she gets caught up in mess with these low life men and I always have to bail her out.

"I'm here to ask you for your blessings on our marriage. I heard that since your pops passed away last year that Jaya looks up to you like ol' pops."

"True and true enough, so what's your profession?"

"I'm a pharmacist."

"Oh true, where you work."

"CVS"

"Okay, I hear you. So are you originally from Tampa because I haven't seen you before?"

"Nawh, you couldn't have seen me. I'm from Miami," revealing his mouth filled with gold's.

After a while I just had to shake my head and put two and two together, drug dealer. My sister is known for attracting some scums of the earth. But I have to give it to her this brother looks like he got money. I just can't jump the gun and not give the brother a chance.

"So how long have you been a pharmacist?"

"For five years, I graduated from the University of Miami."

"Oh true, I can understand that."

"Yeah, I worked my butt off to get where I am at this point."

"Well in the city of beautiful women, why Jayla?"

"I never met a woman like Jaya she gives and treats me like a man should be treated. Your family did a superb job with this God given angel."

"Oh word. So you really haven't told me anything. I know game and I'm not about to have just anyone with my little sister."

"It's okay Ron, I met his entire family. His mom adores me and she told him that he best keep me."

"So which part of Miami are you from?"

"Aventura, but spent most of my time with cousins down in Liberty City and OpaLocka. Dade County all day."

Looking with fire in my eyes at Jaya, "Did you ask the ol' lady?"

"No"

"Well you sure messing up!" You came to the wrong person first. If the ol' gal says it's alright then I'm alright with it." Lord just bless me with only sons because I would have to kill someone over my daughters.

"Grilled chicken, side of smashed potatoes, and cheese covered broccoli . . . Chicken salad . . . prime rib on smashed potatoes and broccoli," the waitress said as she placed food on the table.

"Jaya you do the honor of blessing the table," Lloyd said.

"You know, I really lost my appetite this one is on me." I said as I got up from the table.

Growing up the eldest doesn't always mean that you have all the answers to all problems encountered by your siblings. My parents always made sure I was doing something active. They had me in the Boy Scouts to keep me from getting into trouble, even when I was the only spectacle in the group.

Then when I went to elementary school I tried to talk to other black children my peers, I was considered white or geeky, just because I was proper. I was labeled geeky, just for having my homework done and being the top student in each class. You're talking about being an outcast. There was nothing like not having friends of my own peers. But somehow some way I made it through.

Looking back all the class clowns and the pretty boys or hip crew in high school were either strung out on drugs, locked up or struggling to make ends meet. Looking back over some of their lives it seemed that the cycle of life continued in which their parents had lived. But who am I to judge my family structure was great.

Pops would always tell me that trouble was easy to get into but hard to get out of. By middle school mama was always pushing me in sports. That was also where they both jumped in and taught me the importance and value of money because you never know what headache could come up and you need something to go back and reach for money in a stored, untouched account. Forget about the high school cheerleaders, mama had her custom made jersey with my name and number. She had her pom-poms and cheering crew. It was a few friends of hers and some of her sisters. Uncle Al came out every now and then. Grandma and Poppa came when there were championships. Growing up was great for me. Not saying that my family was great because I do remember constantly going on fishing trips with my Pops when my parents would argue or Pops needed some air.

Chapter 7

Being a member of 100 Black Men has given me the drive to help out in my community. Bringing my mentee, little boys that I mentor, around the life lifestyle that I'm in exposes them to a new way of thinking. I feel great because I have given back. If the children are our future, how they will know that they don't have to be the next rapper, and girls don't have to take off their clothes or succumb to pressure just to make a living? Having built up myself respect along with having wisdom engrained in me from my parents and grandparents is making many tremendous changes in the lives of my mentee's.

I'm just proud to say Terrance Harris from the College Hill neighborhood has graduated with a 3.5 GPA from King High School and has been accepted into Harvard University Minority Scholarship Program. That boy took me for a ride. His mom worked two jobs and his father left them before he was born. This boy started hanging with the wrong crowd of boys and his mom gave me the permission to shake him up. So I just took him to a real prison and let him see where his life was going to end if he keeps on going in the direction that he was headed.

Just for his graduation present I gave him a Mercedes Benz, just like my parents gave me when I graduated high school. What a wonderful feeling. I just had to give Mom's a call and tell him what I was doing. Terrance was smiling from T to T. He being pretty much set, college tuition paid for, new environment, and a fresh set of wheels. Feels like he's my own son . . . .

LaKesha looking at herself in the mirror, Humm, I hope Ron is going to be on his game tonight . . . I just don't want to show him up in a game of pool playing with his friends or not . . .

So humid and hot . . . a night of pool was the right indoor activity on this Friday night . . . . I never been inside this new pool hall that Ron introduced me to . . . . It seems to look like it is packed in the middle of the week. A girl like me never would have thought about this spot . . . All you could see on the outside was nice cars . . . I'm not talking about just any car I'm talking about luxury cars, like Lexus', BMWs and Benz, but a girl these day can't be too picky because these men want to know what you really about . . . Are you a gold digger or not. By the look of things, I really don't care I am going home with the man of my dreams and he has no problem on how I'm looking . . . . Walking through the door greeted by a gust of Newport cigarettes in the air and cigars . . . . I tell you this truly is a man's paradise . . . I really didn't know where I was going but . . . standing in these hills because they are taking a toll on my calves . . . I hope he just come on . . . I can hardly see him through all these fumes . . . oh looking to the right and fanning the smoke from my eyes . . . I walked over to the pool table where all Ron and his home entourage where . . . all looking at me checking me out . . . Ron was like, "Alright fellas just close your mouths . . . this is LaKesha, my lady . . .

Looking at one another nodding as I approached, huge smiles just came across their faces . . . here we go . . . . Just a little kitten surrounded by nothing but dogs . . . Taking a deep breath just to keep the anxiety down . . . Ron came to my side and gave me a kiss, "Hi honey . . ."

"Hi Sweetie . . . how are you?"

"Fellas this is LaKesha"

"Good evening"

With a smirk on my face, "So who's leading and who's just need to go home?"

Looking to each other with laughs and smiles . . ."Well we can say, La'Gwuan just needs to hang it up and go home . . . and rolling their eyes, "Ron is the man."

La'Gwuan, "I don't know why we even come out; Ron always just takes the board."

Laughing with a smile from T to T, "Yeah ya'll have to most definitely have to come a little harder than that," stepping back with his hands in the air . . ."I know how to handle mine, if I must say."

"Here we go," Kevin said.

"Well, I would have to put someone in his place . . . but I'll just be a good woman and sit to the side and let the old man have his day . . ."

Oooohhhhh . . .

"I like this one Ron, she's a little feisty, Mark stated

"Ummm hum maybe a little too much for your hands," Ron stated.

Going back to the table, honey I'm just going to wrap this one up . . . with his confidence just hitting the wall . . .

3 hours passed . . .

Walking to the other side of the room . . . it had turned into a party . . . It was like I was in the middle of the Caribbean . . . looking to the side I seen one of my one night stands along with another former date that I had . . . just let me sit here and drink like they don't see me . . .

"Hi LaKesha," said this one minute wonder . . .

Oh damn, I hope he don't come over here acting like we can make something happen . . . "Not my fault that Mr. Oscar couldn't rise to the occasion . . . he should have taken some Yohimbe, Horny Goat Weed, Damiana or something." I already told him . . . 3-4 inches, width along with fitting a magnum extra-large is only going to cut it . . . I have exceptions but you really have to come to the par with that also . . .

"Long time no chat?"

"Cliff? How are you?

"Fine and as you always are looking."

Blushing . . . , "hummm what brings you my way tonight?

"What else will but a diamond in the middle of a farm?"

"Ha ha ha no you didn't, how you figure."

"You know you are over here just glowing at the bar? So I thought it was just me causing it since I seen you take a look at me?"

Blushing even harder, "Wow ha ha . . . if you say so."

"Say so, I know so"

"Ummm," I hope Ron get's his ass over here and rescue me.

"Can I buy a drink, if that's not too much for you?"

"Humm, well you know this is all I can handle for tonight?"

"Oh . . . excuse me . . . what? I can't believe that one . . . Not Kesha, I Drink a little either this or that?"

"Yes, well you know . . . times change and I can't win them all?" Umm shouldn't have said that . . .

Tugging at my side I just jumped like oh shit he touched the rolls; a deep familiar voice came to my attention, "Hi honey . . ." Oh shit . . . Mr. One night arrogant mother fucker . . . Ron better come and get me . . .

"Hold up, hold up, hold up she with me!" My One night

Mr. Oscar getting all roused up, "I didn't see you put a ring on it breast!"

"Good Evening fella's, Kesha are you ready to go honey?"

Giving him the eye and jumping out of my seat like it was a hot cakes, "yes," he's going to pay for this one . . . had me sitting and doing a two-step every now and then a two-step, "ohhh you are going to get it."

Chapter 8

Block Party

Arising from a Jacuzzi like he was superman, Julian had this sudden urge to get out of town and explore the jungle. It had been a long time since he could go somewhere without any trouble. Paying off his probation officer, he was given the freedom to party out of town with only the restriction of coming back in town before 6AM in the morning.

Looking at his athletic build through the mirror, "Its Julian Jenkins time right now to show my natural ass," Julian said as he danced like an Alpha male.

Reaching for his cell phone, "Hey Steve call the crew we are about to head to the O."

Before going they had decided to meet up at Dejavu so that they could drop some dollars at some strippers.

It was 12 o'clock and no one was really at Roxy's just yet. Those boys from the block had showed up so that they could get a glimpse of chicks coming in through the door.

I and a couple of my home boys from Tampa had decided to go to Orlando just to see who our next victims would be. We were scoping the scene for some project chicks with low self-esteem and that was down for whatever.

1 hour passed

Sound from Rated R's 'I'm not supposed to be in here tonight,' filled the air.

"Damn where is your woman?" This girl came up on me.

"I'm good ma, you're defiantly not my type, but you can keep it moving!"

"Mother fucker you ain't all that!"

"Hoe please!"

Looking at Steve, Could you believe she rolled up on me like that? She looked like she bypassed the mirror for a few days. Her ass looked like she collected a gold mine in her teeth. Shit ain't no way I would get with someone that dirty.

"Well give or take she was bold enough to come flirt with you," Darren said with a questionable look on his face.

"Yeah but I'm not the only mother fucker in here either."

"You know we were just coming in here to find some victims. Damn just get the number, tell them what the deal is and call it a day," Roland with his gangsta mood.

The Motto by Drake came on right in . . ."Everyday Everyday yeah we did roll up here with one mission in mind. Yeah we are on point because I don't see anyone else pulled up in BMW's, Maybacs, or the 300 yet . . . shit let me go on the prowl."

"This mother fucker must not be equipped with the knowledge of the game?" Darren said to Roland.

"Yeah, he'll learn though," Roland said as he sat back at the bar.

Chapter 9

I SEE YOU KNOCKING AND HELL YOU AIN'T COMING IN

Julian was sleeping in his bed from a hangover from Roxy's in Orlando. How in the world? I must have been really fucked up. It was eight in the morning.

KNOCK KNOCK KNOCK

He picked up the phone, "Hello . . . . Hello. He then looked at his phone seeing that it was put on silence, and that he had missed 5 calls.

GRANDMA

MOMMA

PBITCH

PBITCH

UNAVAILABLE

KNOCK KNOCK KNOCK

He knew that it had to be someone that didn't know him or something. Everyone knew that in order to contact me they were going to have to call after 10AM. He didn't go to the door but looked at his home security monitor and saw that it was two police officers. Back in his mind he knew that they couldn't come in without a warrant.

KNOCK KNOCK KNOCK

The police officers looked at each other and headed back for their cars.

Lying back into bed, "Crooked ass cops. Ain't up to no damn good."

Chapter 10

I received a call from Jennifer. “Mr. Jenkins I have some good news and bad news for you. Which one do you want to hear first?” She asked.

“Give me the bad, so that I can know the damage first, and heal me with the good.” I said as I lay in the bed with this huge hang over.

“Are you alright?”

“Yeah, recuperating from some guests I had in this weekend.”

“Well sir, you never got back with me in regards to where you wanted the company to go for this quarter so the company just went down $10 million in revenues.”

“Oh Shit, excuse my French Jennifer.”

“Yes . . . I tried getting in contact with you on multiple occasions. Are you sure you’re okay Mr. Jenkins? You don’t seem the same.”

“Well Jennifer, there has been a lot on my plate.”

“Oh, I’m sorry to hear that sir. Is there anything I can do to help?”

“No . . . I’ll manage”

“Okay”

“I knew that there was going to be an influx of companies changing over to Indian Accountants. I just didn’t prepare myself.”

“Yes, that’s what I’m hearing under the table these days. I just don’t know how American businesses are going to survive with all these jobs being out sourced to India.”

“Well, Jennifer it’s called kiss it until you can kick it. I just have to get ready for this globalizing of business.”

“I hear that, by the number . . . yeah you need to do something and do it quickly.”

"Yeah, I know time is of an essence."

"It's your call sir."

"Jennifer, please get together my board members, we need to get together and have a meeting."

"Okay"

"I need some pressing issues to be presented, old news, information on the sudden moves of our competitors, if we need to upgrade our systems. I need to know how each branch is doing. Give me the facts and the numbers."

"Right on it sir"

"And Jennifer what do you have to heal me before I head to lunch with Maurion."

"Well Sir, your branch of J credit cards is on an all-time high. People are going to prepaid cards to save themselves from FRAUD. I need to set up a date with your accountant so that you can go over your financial portfolio. Do you have a date that you think would be feasible with your schedule?"

"Yes, make that Monday at 12 noon. That's my day to sit back."

Chapter 11

On a lunch break one day one of my new accountants, Maurion Duncan, had offered to take me out for a bite. Trying to make sure he had the job. What a thoughtful way to keep my pressure of work off of him. It was quite a surprise that when we came around the corner off of 7th Avenue to Channelside drive, it was like a whole new world tucked away on the water. There were many restaurants in the area, but I had decided to go to the Thai restaurant. It was something entirely new for me. My eyes opened up into more of an awwh when we went through the doors from Western society being clutched in the arms of Thailand. The greeters wore beautiful Thailand attire and then looking all around it was just spectacular. Never in my life had I seen such architecture of the furniture carved out to form like Thai art. It was simply beautiful.

Maurion Duncan was a recent graduate from the University of South Florida. GO BULLS my Alma Mater. He was the top in his class, making him very smart. This brother had it together at such a young age. He reminded me much of myself. Last summer he was a part of an internship brought on by the school and was one out of six to successfully make it through my internship. What a pleasant surprise that he had come back to begin his career in accounting at my firm.

Chapter 12

Back at the office looking out on the city from my office, I just couldn't believe that this world is changing so fast . . . I really want to be ahead of things but it's like a continuous cycle. Seems like the harder I go trying to place things in perspective and in their proper place a monkey wrench is always thrown in my direction or at my family. Well they did say that life is about change and if you don't change you simply die. Being out here trying to make deals being the middle man can be a hard task at times because there will always be another business opening up with the same services and how things are now taxes and all important documenting or financial record keeping jobs are being out sourced to China. I don't have a problem with India or global expansion but how much power you give another when not looking out for those that represents home. I look out for all my employees and make sure that they are given the best opportunities available along with giving them $1000 stipend when going to college; this company may be the stepping stone for another career.

Noon already

"Mr. Jenkins there is a man here from the IRS that has to speak with you."

"Okay send him in"

This cocky guy came in the door with this disappointing look on his face, "Yes, I'm Peter Tucker with the IRS, your company has been called into Fraud for a temporary freeze. We are investigating your company off of a lead that we received from an anonymous caller."

My heart just sunk into my heart, "Say what? How could this be I have everything in my company back checked through three different sources so that this scenario could not be possible."

"Well Sir we have escorted all of your employees out and they are currently being interrogated."

"Let me call my lawyer."

"No problem, you do have that right, he said as he looked around my office, quite impressive office you have here."

"Jennifer, could you please get Bryant Scriven on the line."

"Already on it Sir."

"See this why I hired you. Good looking out." I stated seeing Jennifer's hand shake as she held the phone to her hear.

"I couldn't believe this myself." Jennifer said.

"Yeah this does not look good for business, advise Maurion that his job is on a freeze until the company gets cleared."

Chapter 13

It's Hot

It was the beginning of the summer, the sun was shining and the smell of the Gulf of Mexico created this relaxing mood. People were having a good time on here Clearwater Beach. The sand gave off this nice warm feeling as the squalling sounds of seagulls echoed back and forth down the beach. Sipping on glasses of Moet, LaKesha and I were sitting in each other's arms as we digested food from Crabby Bills. With my Hawaiian trunks showing off my athletic frame, it was truly getting hot.

Summer was the time when you see some of the oddest type bodies and the oddest couples gathered all on the beach having a good time. Snowbird's would drive down and get their feel of the beautiful Florida weather. Tourists were coming from all parts of the world driving like they lost their mind or like there was no tomorrow. You had made many options of enjoying Florida. There was Disney World, Bush Gardens, Adventure Island, Anna Maria Island, Honey Moon Island, Madeira, Sea World, Universal Studios, Clearwater Beach, Siesta Key, The Keys, Miami, West Palm Beach, Panama City and the list goes on. I had a wonderful time with LaKesha she was fun to be around. I think is a great idea to take her out again. I don't want to rush fast in the deal because if I go to fast I'll spoil it all. The thing is I want to appreciate her. I also want her to appreciate the different aspects of my personality. There are days when I have to balance my spirit. There would be nights when I spend my Fridays at the Fox to listen to some nice Jazz or whatever good music the band had to offer. Then I might just want to spend my time in solitude at night just walking the beach. Whether its day or night the thrill of a little fishing from St. Petersburg Pier gets my adrenalin going and I feel like a true warrior for catching a 50 pound Red Snapper. Along with being an athlete in high school I just love getting my adrenaline going through kick boxing and running. There are times when I feel like James Brown and I have to jump back and kiss myself and enjoy my soul through poetry or Island Vibez, Black on Black Rhymes or Soulful Expressions. Then again I like to balance myself with some Chi Kung-Tai Chi and Yoga.

The weather in Florida would change on all levels. One day it's beautiful, next day it rains, few weeks could go by and there is a cold snap, after that you have more thunder storms, and finally you're back to nothing but beautiful sunny weather.

LaKesha wore this two piece bathing suit . . . . umm. The bra just coupled her breast and it looked as though someone had spray painted on her thong onto her lower body when she took off her wrap.

"Baby you have something to cover that up?" I asked.

"Ha . . . cover what?"

"You know what I mean!"

With a smirk on her face, "Well baby this is all, I have I am California Beach baby you remember."

"I don't want some other man seeing what I have."

"Well baby it's not a mystery." She chuckled, "I am a woman!"

"Baby just put on the wrap you brought," I said.

Bending over showing every inch of her ass, she replied, "whatever you want baby."

"Girl you almost made me nut right out here on the beach."

"Ummm Hummm, that's what I know."

"Isn't this nice," LaKesha said jumping through the shallow water.

"Yes but I want to go see what's going on over at the pier. We have plenty of time to come back."

Reaching the pier there were vendors selling beach souvenirs as we passed couples kissing on benches. There were a couple of men fishing. Many families were walking back and forth through the entrance of the pier looking at beach collectibles sold by vendors.

"You want some ice cream?" I asked.

"Yes, I'll have some."

Entering the doors to the restaurant there was just an array of ice-creams to choose from. The line was so long, but we seemed to have our two scoops of strawberry cheese cake ice cream cones out in ten minutes. As we made our way out the door into the pavilion it was the perfect timing to hear a group of performers from Jamaica playing there steel drums as they revamped Bob Marley's hits. The small area was filled with many tourists and white people dancing like they had lost their minds. When I say they were getting it. They were getting it. I don't understand how they had so much energy; because how they were moving their bodies you would have thought they would be tired.

"Baby let's dance." LaKesha demanded.

"Okay I'm going to tell you I haven't danced in a while."

"So . . . I will show you."

2 MINUTES PASSED

I ran back toward the seat. Just gasping for breath, "Shoot baby you ain't tired yet?"

"No . . . . have you forgotten that this 26 year old, dark chocolate thick young lady has time to be tired?"

"I tell you . . . you know what? I'm not going to let you showcase me . . . . Let's go back to the floor." Knowing by the time I get back to my house I will need to soak my body in Alexyss K Taylor's Pain Ointment guaranteed to get my muscles warmed up and moving . . . and some of Judah's Gold Pain reliever spray.

"Let me let you rest your old tired body down," LaKesha said as she laughed at me.

Walking the beach as the sun set was simply beautiful. Just exhaling, I have found someone that I can truly spend the rest of my life with. It became dark.

Popping a mosquito off her leg, "Baby let's head back before some creepy crawlies start crawling up my legs please."

"Well we don't have to go back in town?"

"You have the weekend off right?"

Looking at me with a smirk, "Yes"

"Well I have secured us an ocean view at the hotel."

"Really" LaKesha said with a huge grin across her face.

We grabbed our belongings from the beach. I took the keys from my back pocket and put on my wife beater on and we headed back to my white BMW convertible and headed toward the hotel. I let the top down and LaKesha's hair just blew in the wind. It was a beautiful evening.

Reaching the beautiful guest suite with rose pedals leading to the bed, LaKesha covered me with kisses. Now I was a horny as hell. It had been two weeks of dodging each other that I had to have some. The beach had worn me out, but shit. I know I had enough energy left to tear that pussy up. Maybe LaKesha can take it this time but one thing I know I just have to let go of this built up pressure that's in me. This time the real rude side of me was coming out as if I was the center feature in a Black Cherry flick. Hell if she doesn't know right now that it's all for whatever going down in here tonight.

Having me almost nut on the beach as she flaunted that fat pussy of hers; at this moment payback is a bitch right about now. Almost the question of whether she can handle all of me for two hours really makes me guess?

"You can take off all of your clothes right now."

Smiling with a seductive look across her face, "You ain't said nothing but a word."

Pulling back the sheets I threw LaKesha's body on to the bed. "Are you ready for this?"

"Yes big daddy, I have been waiting for this moment. I have packed twelve of my Fredrick's and Victoria Secrets lingerie in my luggage.

Twenty-four different sessions of making love and the thought of making this girl my wife could be a notion . . . . Kissing her all over her body was my mission to make this a foreplay that LaKesha would never have experienced before.

"Baby I like it hard . . . harder please."

Thrusting in and out of her pussy like turbine engines ready to move a train. It was as if a beast had risen up out of me like none other. I started given her some of my special Tantra loving; flipping her body over for my special K-9 position listening to her moaning and groaning as she laid her head between two pillows . . . doing my shallow and deep thrusts in concessions, working it from side to side, up and down. I began pulling her hair, "How do you like that?"

"Baby give me some more"

30 minutes passed SHIT. I have met my match. My muscles in my lower back began to spasm but damn that pussy was good. Flipping her over, I placed one of her legs over my arm. Pounding just giving it to her, it was like I hadn't done a thing to her. She still wanted more.

"Shit baby give it to me oooohhhh . . . there's something that I have to tell you."

"Shit not right now you don't."

"Baby, I'm a freak, some sort of a nympho."

'Umm Hummm . . . . Hummm."

Another 30 minutes passed then she placed her legs behind her head. Oh damn. I felt my leg about to go into a cramp. "Baby I'm catching a cramp." Stopping for a moment to release the cramp, I snatched LaKesha's body from the bed and onto the dresser. Kissing her nipples then her, DAMN baby, I climaxed.

Lying on my back on the bed, "Baby come and do your special work for me," I said making her walk to the bed from the bathroom. Ten minutes of nothing but fire ass head. Shit, jumping up my dick hard as hell. She lay on the bed and then placed both of her legs behind her head like a diamond again. I couldn't help but beat it up some more.

"AWWWHHH SHIT!!!!" I screamed as LaKesha untied her legs and forced me on my back. For the next hour she rode me . . . oh shit turning her body around back facing me she began to twirk it. For the next ten minutes . . . .

"Ohhhhhhh baby I'm about to explode," she screamed.

"Explode then . . . shit." That was a vaginal ejaculation; I am going for clitoris orgasms though. It is the watery ejaculate that sprays or gushes out . . . Skeet, skeet, skeet!

She began to slow up . . . . Next minute she was back at it again . . . I thought she would have had enough.

"Baby you have some fire ass head."

Got her locked in, "Oh yeah"

"Yes baby you doooo." Sounding like Scooby she climaxed two more times in a row, having a full body orgasm, her whole body spasmed as she completely surrendered to me.

Let me give her a minute. Five minutes that is . . . .

Chapter 14

Finding my ass

Man that LaKesha is something else. The thoughts of making love to her cross my mind every 15 seconds. She made my favorite breakfast before she left for work today. I think I'm just going to take it easy today and work from home.

"Ahhh OhhLawwwd." Rising out of my custom made king size bed I almost tripped on my pants on my way to the balcony. I put on my bathrobe and picked up my laptop. LaKesha put my breakfast in a covered dish by the door. So I just yawned as I reclined in patio furniture overlooking the bay.

Booting up my Apple, I searched through my company's information. The results from the last quarter for June were in. Revenue for the quarter was $675.9 million compared to $380.7 for the same period last quarter. Net income for the quarter $15 million compared to the net loss of $2.5 million for the third quarter last year.

I have many ventures to think about especially with the new buzz of outsourcing work. I can invest in some other companies to bring me back some revenue. I started out the day thinking of how much money I could accumulate so that I could retire early. It was said that a Black man couldn't live past the age of 65 without dying from diabetes and high blood pressure. Then to live past the age of twenty five without any children or locked up in jail was a cry of a miracle.

Well standing at 6'4, 220 pounds this dark, suave, and debonair young man at the age of 35, I had beaten all the odds. Hummm . . . . I wonder if I could at least cash in my Boeing stock would I be left with a cool $100 billion if I was pressed on my last savings? Considering the fact those years before I lost over $500 million in stocks invested in Enron. Stock options were something that I needed to take up with my financial accountant. I scheduled a meeting Thursday at three o'clock at the local 5/3 Bank located in downtown Tampa. Yes I have cash in the bank but wanted to make sure I kept it in balance of what was going on in the world and what I wanted to take pleasure in at the drop of a hat. Though that IRS audit raised my sugar so high felt like I was about to go into a heart attack everything just happened so fast. But what happened to me, the energy from a good woman just takes all the edge off. Like any other man . . . . I love me some chocolate and my own supply is the love I receive from LaKesha.

June had gone by with a reluctant pass of Father's Day. I don't know how my mother was doing this time around. She had always taken our Pops out on a fishing trip down in Daytona. But it seems that she has not gotten over it. I didn't hear a word from her so I just assumed that everything was okay. The more I began to think about if it would it be right to take the next step with LaKesha or not. I just really didn't know. I never had feelings like this until I had my first love. But the question seemed to beat me down. I really didn't want no one to know what my next moves where, in particular, my family.

At times I felt like making my proposal to LaKesha but I really didn't know how she would take it. If I moved too fast on her she might end up being a gold digger or something. I really don't know what her mission is between us but this girl has given me the vibes. It's almost as if I can't go a day without hearing from her. My ass done went crazy by going to Victoria's secret and buying a bottle of Very Sexy and putting it on to a pillow on my bed just to know that I'm in love. That pillow comes handy every now and then when our schedules become too busy. Both of us having busy work schedules I just hope that it doesn't get in the way of our love. One thing I truly know is that if you don't take care of home someone else will. Considering the facts, LaKesha knows what type of man I am, so my frequent trips out of town shouldn't bother her at all.

"Baby I'll be leaving soon?"

"Say what? Where? When? And how long?"

"Well you know I'm just going for a month. I have to go out of town and check out some new ventures for my company in Atlanta. Check out their annual skating Skate Jam and Competition which is only held in September. Then I'll be back home."

"And who is going to be accompanying you?"

"Jennifer, my personal assistant."

"Humm"

"Baby you don't have anything to be worried about, Jennifer is good peoples, and I put her in her place years ago. My pops always told me, "Never mix business with pleasure."

"So am I pleasing you enough?"

"Honey you are a bundle of pleasure, I'll never let you go."

Rubbing the back of her fingers against my chin, "Oh is that right?"

Looking her in her eyes, I just knew that she was the right one for me.

I just had this bad feeling about leaving Julian at my house, but this he is my brother.

Chapter 15

Mr Peacock!

Returning home for Mom's birthday party felt so great. On my way to Rowlett Park, hours before the big day for ol' girl. I decided to stop by Aunty Louise's house before going to the party. Aunty Louise the great Aunt of the family she knew everything that went on in the family. Know why—because she was there—right in the midst of it all.

"Come here boy, I haven't seen you in a while where have you been?" She asked in an excited voice as if she was still living in her 20's.

"You know Aunty I have to pay those bills. You know I heard someone always quoting if a man doesn't work, he doesn't eat." I said.

"You right about that baby and who told you that, and where did it come from son?" Aunty Louise said raising her eyebrows with a smirk on her face.

Standing up as if I was behind a pulpit, "From the Bible, and transferred into the mouth of none other than the mouth of Aunty Louise!"

"You got that right baby. That's what the word says, that what the word say." Aunty Louise said with a chuckle.

You know how it goes if you are born into a family everyone expects for you to act a certain way. Yeah, just because you have an older brother it doesn't mean that the younger siblings will want to grow up in the same image that he or she has.

"This mother fucker thinks that he is the gift to the whole entire world," Julian mumbles to himself about Ron as he walks into his mom's birthday party the family was throwing at Rowlett Park.

Yeah Julian was truly Ron's spitting image. It was just like how in the world could two different siblings look identical to each other both born one child apart. It was a hot day in Tampa. Everyone was expecting it to rain since it was right dead in center of the summer. It rained two days in a row before Saturday. It was told on ABC Action News that there was going to be a slight chance of rain going to be taking place later on this Saturday morning. There was a cool breeze coming through the park as I stepped out of my SUV.

It was a beautiful day. The sight of smoke coming from Uncle Al's barbeque grill had caused this bubbling sound to pass through my stomach. There were balloons everywhere and children running around in the field, playing horse-shoes in the middle of the open area. All the Thomas's, some Jenkins and friends of the family and Mom's former co-worker's was gathering for the special occasion. The celebration was supposed to start at 2pm, but you know CPT time. In case you didn't know Colored People Time seemed to run quite often for many of our family functions. The event just wasn't going to be right if all family members came in at the same time. The most successful ones or the ones that thought they had their shit together had to be seen trying to show up fashionably late. You know there always had to be a gossip section formed by a few aunties and Big Mamma. Thank God I sent in for catering so that I could participate in the giving, finding it hard to understand how people show up to event's empty handed.

"What's up Uncle Al?" I stated.

"Nothing much there boy, just que'n on this grill you know how I do it."

Uncle Al stood about 5'9 and straight white gray hair all over his head. Looking like Morgan Freeman's twin. He was the true street hustler. He owned a couple of night clubs down in Ybor City back in his time and continues to run his own restaurant down off of 40th street. When it is time to do business no matter on what level, Uncle Al had his stuff together. I wouldn't call him a womanizer or anything because women just seemed to flock to him. I have to give it to him, he has a genuine heart and that's just something that you don't see in most people these days. For some odd reason he had a different story for every occasion. You couldn't just leave the table because the emotions that he put into the story just had you caught up to find out what else happened. When you have a person that has been places and experienced things a person should listen so that they will not make the same mistakes. But like my Popps always said, "People that don't listen feel."

"Well you know what I'm about to do?" Let you do what you do Unc" I stated with this grin across my face.

"What's up little Bra."

With a chip on his shoulder, "Ain't nothing, what's going on with you?" Julian asked.

"Shit, just chilling. You know I had to come out and show my support for ol'-girl"

"Yeah, true, true, same here."

"So when was the last time I seen you?"

"It's been about a month. You know we passed each other the other day. You were headed west on Busch in your white on white magnum, and I was headed North on Nebraska in my new red and black magnum."

"Oh for show"

"Well you know I have to be one foot behind you in the latest styles. It may take me a while . . . . You know you have to crawl before you walk.

"You're not lying about that."

Jaya strolls in with her new man, smiling from T to T, "Greetings everyone this Lloyd."

Everyone turned and looked and gave their nods of greetings and turned back around.

Silence set in between both of us since I was the eldest child and a few years older. I had moved out of the house when Julian was growing up. There was really no connection but through our parents. I really didn't have time for him. I had attended college full time at the University of South Florida and went straight into the family business once I finished my internship at JP Morgan and Chase. When you're a man about your business you have to make things happen or they will not happen at all. In the midst of making things happen, you neglect the things around you whether it is family, friends or your own personal day-to-day activities. Something has to give or you could end up stuck on the same thing years down the line on a project that was only intended for a month.

I regret missing time with Julian, but the Jenkins image in accounting I have to uphold. Dealing with my own personal issues of not having a woman and children at this particular point in my life is really sending me into panic mode.

Julian, on the other hand, was just particularly spoiled by my mother. This was her period to make up for the time she had left me and the Jaya to pursue her own life of independence. Creating her own monster, she couldn't control how Julian acted anymore. Yeah, he stood an inch shorter than me but some of his characteristics just don't seem to match up. He's very passive and always trying to fit in with the craziest people. Being born into a rich family just doesn't mean that you will get along with everyone. You tend to have your haters and your users. People just for some strange reason hating on you because of what you have, then trying to use what you have to make themselves feel better.

Walking through the grass I heard the clicking of the horse-shoes. I started laughing as I seen Malcolm making circles around the pole with his horse shoe.

"Ya'll don't know anything about playing horse-shoes."

"Yeah, and you don't know how to grow up Uncle Ron," Terrance said.

"Ha HaHaaaaa," I couldn't hold back the laughs.

"You know that your old body will snap and pop. Don't eat too much of Uncle Al's cooking. We don't want to have to call 911 because I'm not in no kind of way putting my mouth on another man's mouth ewwwh." Malcolm said as he motioned to throw his last horse shoe.

"See there, you don't even have the right focus or concentration to even complete your move."

"Whatever."

All the family was sitting at the table laughing and cracking on each other at the picnic table. "Boy you know you crazy," one cousin blurted out with laughter. Focusing my attention on Julian, I had decided to again break the ice, "so how are things going with your car?"

Out of nowhere Julian just went off and attacked me, "How in the hell are you going to sit up here and ask me a question like that. You act like you pay my bills, put food on my table and put the clothes on my back. Don't anyone in this family do shit for me. Rising out of his chair, Julian left the table and looked me dead in my face.

By this time the entire scene went to Julian and me.

"Dude, calm down. I wasn't even trying to poke fun at you or anything I was just simply asking you a question. I stated with a calm manner and demeanor."

"Yeah, whatever you think you're all that since you graduated from USF, got your own car and crib, but mother fucker you ain't shit," Julian stated as he motioned towards me.

IMMEDIATELY COMING BETWEEN US . . . .

Uncle Al put down his spatula, "Ya'll ain't even got to take it this way. Julian you know it's your mom's birthday, let us put the attention on her. You know your brother was just playing with you. Go take your ass somewhere and walk it off Julian."

"It ain't over," Julian stated looking at me.

"Yes, the hell it is boy. Didn't I tell you to walk it over, don't let me have to pull out my belt. You ain't too grown to still get your ass whipped," Uncle Al stated as he pointed in the direction for Julian to walk.

Walking away from the celebration and onto the trail, "Man this some bull," Julian said as he pulled out his phone calling his friend T. "Yeah man, I'm tired of my older brother. That mother fucker just crossed the wrong person. I know you know how to set him up. I just won't be involved. I'll pay you for it." He walked causally down by the river to blow off steam.

"Man, why he had to play me like he did? He'll never want to fuck with me again. I don't like people fucking with me. Don't they understand that it's serious with me?" Pacing back and forth round the bank, "how on earth are things going to happen like this he my blood but I can't stand that mother fucker?"

One thing about a mother watching her children fighting against each other can hurt her heart. There were her boys showing out on her birthday like clowns. What an embarrassment. How in the world could things go down like they did? Knowing all the years she went on providing for her family, she had to live for her right now. It was time spent since she had to bail Julian out of jail, pay for his child support just so that he wouldn't go back to jail, taking over all of his responsibilities just until he had found another job. At the rate he was going she knew that further down the line Julian was going to get into something that he wouldn't be able to get himself out of. So this time he was going to have to live life without this Ol' lady's help.

A mother's intuition compounded with a woman's courage to stand and do what she had to do. Two months had passed and like anticipated Julian got into something else this time it was something minor. He forgot to check in with his probation officer. He had switched from the last one and found himself with the nastiest woman. She had the absolute worst woman's scorn for a man. Anything Julian did was simply not good enough.

Chapter 16

The End of a New Beginning

It had been a long November. I was just finishing up the day I wanted to be extra prepared for this new quarter. I had new projections for the coming year and I wanted to present them to the board members to get their thoughts and ideas. It was around 9:30PM and we wrapped things up. It's something about crunching numbers; the shit can cause you to mentally collapse. I need to schedule a massage at La Cri Bella Spa and just chill out for the weekend. I'm not about to allow this job to kill me.

The month of traveling had placed many demands on me. LaKesha just kept calling me with the anticipation that I would just be able to fly back in. How would I be able to tell her that it may look like I would have to be out for another month? She'll be alright, I trust her to make a sound decision. Shit, her ass best go and get a dildo or something just to hold her off until I come back.

The only thing I could do was talk to her when I was free. It was like the only thing I could do. I had flowers delivered to her at the end of each week. I know her girlfriends or co-workers would be hating on her.

Reaching home that night, just as I was hitting the door, the sound of Rated Next's "You are my high" echoed through the PA system. There was a savor of collard greens, oxtails, and God knows whatever else just reeking in the air.

I went towards the kitchen to find LaKesha sitting on top of the table in this silk black robe with a corset, stilettos and pinned up stockings. She handed me a glass of Cristal.

"Drink baby"

"Humm will do"

"I love you"

"Oh you do?"

Here we were again on the top of the kitchen table. Pushing her panties to the side . . . .

The rays of the sun and sounds of bird's chirpings awoke me lying in the bed by myself. LaKesha left the area for a few minutes. Hearing her footsteps pace around in the kitchen. She came back to the room with sliced fruits and vegetables.

"Do you love me LaKesha?"

"Waking up at 7a.m. this morning to prepare your breakfast in bed and you ask me a question like that?"

"Do you love me LaKesha?"

"Yes, why?"

Shaking my head, "Just asking."

RING RING RING

"I thought we were supposed to have the weekend to ourselves?"

"Well baby, I just forgot to turn off my phone. I couldn't get to the real reason but I was waiting on a call from the office since it's the end of another quarter. I just turned to the side and turned the phone off.

Damn I thought I turned off the phone. Now I just hope she doesn't trip.

Revealing her Victoria Secret thongs that looked like floss between her ass ummmummm**DAMN**.

"Baby I didn't know you had a birth mark on your thigh."

"Yeah, it tends to fade in and out depends on the season it is. Cool Huh?"

"Yeah"

LaKesha poured me some orange juice as I sat watching CNN and ESPN News. Need to get my update on how Mr. Morris going to make our Buccaneer's head for the Super Bowl. I just sat there in my bed like a king while LaKesha uncovered my breakfast.

"Breakfast in bed?" I asked.

"Yes, anything else for my king?" she asked.

"Yes" I just looked her up and down as she stood next to the bed.

"How do you want me? You know I can strip tease for you Big Daddy?"

The aroma of French Coffee filling the air, I just had to take another sip of my Folgers. I had to keep my man man from getting too wild, I had two plates of hot food and coffee in the middle of my lap. LaKesha had me trapped; she bent over to take her thongs off.

"Stay right there in that position for me." Turn around to the side!"

5 MINUTES PASSED

"Alright baby blood is rushing to my head . . . getting a little dizzy here."

"Oh okay baby you can precede on doing what you were doing."

"Do you need some more syrup for your French toast?"

"No"

"Butter for your grits?"

"No"

Chapter 17

ANOTHER DAY ANOTHER DOLLAR

Ring Ring Ring

Looking at a desk filled with papers Ron closed his eyes and began **scratching** his head. Ron Jenkins how may I assist you . . .

"For one thing you can clear your schedule for the rest of the day and we head down to an already booked room at the Ritz Carlton in Sarasota." LaKesha's soft

A quick smirk and eye opening grin came over my face, "sounds great"

"Yes honey, did I forget to mention that the room is overlooking the sea so we can watch the sunset as your untying my new corset that I bought from Fredrick's.

"Letting out a big breath of air, baby I'm loaded for today," I said sternly.

"Shhhh don't even say another word. I'm already here sitting in bubbles awaiting you as you finish up with what you have to do," LaKesha's succulent voice just cooing me on the way.

"Ummm, pushing away from my desk, placing my feet on the edge of the desk, "So tell me how's my sugar pie doing?" I asked trying to divert the attention to the suggestion. Though taking a break from these creditors and this stress could do my diabetes some good. I do need to relax.

"Well right now she's warm after taking a nice soak in a warm bath and just waiting for your company."

"Has she gotten tight since . . . ? Well I just need to know, has my sugar pie has been taken care of?"

"Humm, I knew I could get you in the mood for this new trick that I have learned with some cherry's and whipped cream . . . so we both are awaiting you."

KNOCK KNOCK KNOCK

"Yes?" I questioned my secretary.

"Mr. Jenkins, I have all your paper work done, all we need is your final approval so that we can finish out the books?"

"Well, I'll catch up with you later," I stated to her.

"Handle your business baby I'll be waiting. Need I mention that my new striptease class that I have been taking."

"Will do"

5 hours later

The sweet smells of pineapple soy candles from Nubian Essence the crunching of red peddles leading to LaKesha laying on the bed. An open bottle of Moet and the voice of R. Kelly's touched a Dream filled the room. Umm my lips touching a very sexy neck . . . nip and suck followed by the soft touch of a French kiss. My hands moved down the small of her back. Grasping this plump ass sent an electric impulse through my entire body. I remember watching a DVD by Dr. Jewel Pookrum and she said "Big buttocks equals intellectual capacity." "Damn, LaKesha must be one of the smartest women on the planet?" . . . . Pulling the strings from the corset . . . my eyes awaiting the site of LaKesha's pretty breasts had to be a good 36D in size . . . a little kiss here a little kiss there breathing as my face went between her breasts lifting her body so I had a greater angle at tasting my sweet potato pie . . . . Feeling the dimples against my cheeks . . . I felt like a child at the candy store. Flipping her over on her hands and knees thrashings in and out . . .

BANG BANG BANG

"Ohhh just like that baby." She looked back at me.

"You like that . . . I took a moment and let her pussy yearn for my dick."

"Yes daddy . . . Go harder!!!"

By that time I had the pillows thrown off the bed, "Shit . . ." grasping her hair I began to feel the back of her pelvis. Poppp Poop Pop . . . ," Damn done pulled my back out of place,"

Lifting her medium frame off the bed and onto the dresser . . .

GUSH GUSH GUSH . . .

"Kiss me" . . . she demanded . . . Grasping her breast and kissing her lips . . .

1 hour in . . . Drops of sweat began to move down my back . . .

"Baby I want some more."

She must think I'm the fucking Energizer Bunny. I guess, I could be that's why I practice my Chi Kungs daily. From the dresser I pulled her body and stood her up and made her touch her hands to the ground . . . and I was in there . . . this was some good as pussy . . . I took her body placing her against the wall as I kissed her ears from behind thrusting my dick all in her pussy . . .

"Oh Ohhhh Daddy . . . I like it like that . . . give me some more . . .

I'm in love with a freak . . . I snatched her and went to the balcony . . .

"Baby . . . people are looking."

I was still going hard . . . .

"Baby we are drawing a crowd of old men."

Smiling . . . "Baby they stopped because they wish that they only have what I'm receiving."

"Oh . . . you like that daddy."

Taking her back into the room I just let her do her thing, "so what was that trick you had to show me?"

"I don't know if you are ready for that."

"I have a few more minutes on me."

Going to the refrigerator like I hadn't even touched her, she placed the whip cream around my wood then she pulled a few cherries out of the bag one of which she circled around her lips . . . and slowly began to eat . . . then she placed another one in her mouth. She placed her lips against my dick as she slowly eased him in I felt the uneaten cherries still in her mouth and she slide her tongue around as if she was sucking on a lolly pop. "You want me to come for you baby?"

"Ummm," she moaned as she took the tip of her tongue to the whole of my penis, "are you going to come for me daddy" After 30 minutes, "Here I come baby . . . are you going to swallow." "I asked because, I can't be like Onan in the Bible and waste my seed today.

"Boy you are crazy; if that's what you want me to do daddy," She said.

"Here it comes," Grabbing her head against my wood. Now, when the average male ejaculates, he loses more than 1 tablespoon of semen. The nutritional value is equal to that of two New York steaks, ten eggs, six oranges, and two lemons combined. Ejaculation is often called "coming". Shit! The precise word for it should be "going", because everything—vital energy, millions of live sperms, hormones and nutrients go away.

She swallowed and smiled. As I laid there I just felt her gentle lips kissing all over my chest.

"How was that baby?" she asked . . .

I took her to my side and held her in my arms, "That's was all I needed that was excellent, where did you learn that one from?"

"You know birds of a feather do flock together," she laughed, "can't tell you that one."

"Well, ummm . . . I like that . . . I would like to see what else you like to see what else you have up your sleeve."

"Well since hooking up with Reverend Goddess Charmaine, Trybal Queen and reading Change Your Man by Kenya Stevens . . . we have more to explore," LaKesha said with this big smile on her face.

"Umm, we might have to ride down to Hollywood, Florida and learn some Tantra Techniques from the Grand Master of Tantra himself Sunyata Saraswati."

Kissing me on my lips, "sounds like a plan baby mmm."

Chapter 18

TELEMARKETERS

A New Year and things seemed on track finally. My business had soared through the year while other businesses seemed to collapse. And they thought just because I was a young black male that I would just let my father's business fall after five years of running it. I can just wipe the hateration off my brows and neck because they haven't seen a mother fucker do it like I have done it.

After a grueling first quarter, my companies stocks had risen five times higher than in past years in so short amount of time. Life was a cool breeze at this point everything was going easy. Will this be the year that I need to marry LaKesha or not? I'm not the one to jump the broom so fast. I have too much at stake. Far too much money accumulated at risk. After becoming a member of Hustle University with Hotep and reading Donald Trump's 'How to become rich' books I don't think she will agree to a prenuptial agreement. Yeah all is fair between love and war but my existence with or without this woman is a huge question.

If it weren't a necessity to have a personal assistant at this point I could handle everything on my own. When you finally get things going, seems like life with its infinite changes steps in it seems like one thing happens after another. First, there are creditors calling the phone. For some odd reason it began with one and now it's five. I keep asking myself what on earth did I do to get these calls. I have two credit cards and I have not been late on any of my payments. I checked over the monthly statements online and there is no overuse and oh yeah there is no slight detection of FRAUD.

"Hello is there a Ron home," a soft voice said.

With a polite tone, "This is Ron"

"My name is Lisa calling you from Vasta Credit with an attempt to collect on an outstanding debt." Lisa said with an East Indian accent.

"Well Sir, I am calling you today in regards to an outstanding balance with Larky furniture. Are you prepared to pay this balance of $15,000?"

"$15,000, I can't believe this shit how in the world I have a bill for $15,000 all of my furniture is paid for. I don't have another house to furnish or have furnished."

"Well sir you can make monthly payments to get this balance taken care of."

"Let me think for a second." I said because this call seemed to be going by too fast.

"Well sir it's stated that you made this purchase back in April of 2005 and there was one cash payment made for $1,000 but after that we are showing no other payments made," she said with a patient and polite tone.

I don't know who got my damn information. I might have to beat the shit out of them once I report them to the FBI, police, CIA, or whoever.

"Ma'am, clearly there has been a misunderstanding somehow or somewhere that could not be me." I had to keep my cool because you never know how much help a representative will give you if you catch them in one of their off days.

"Sir, one moment while I look into this for you. Do you live at 9375 Megamy Rd in Tampa, FL?"

"Yes" How in the world.

"Could you please verify your date of birth and social security?"

"Well, I'll be damned. Ma'am I will give you the last four digit of my Social Security because I don't believe in giving out all my personal information over the phone. You can verify with me if the information that I'm giving you matches whatever that's on your computer screen."

"Yes, sir that is the information that I have before me, would you like to make a payment today?"

Ohhh Shit. "No please transfer me to your FRAUD department because I know I haven't purchased anything through your company."

15 MINUTES GOES BY

My ass is still on hold.

"This is Bernard Williams, Fraud representative for Vasta Credit how may I help you today?"

"Yes sir, I am calling in regards to a collection call today. My name in Ron Jenkins, I am attempting to get this situation clarified and settled. I did not make any purchases with your company."

"Sir may I have your social security number?"

"Why yes."

"Well sir I'm showing that there was something purchased in your name in April of 2005 with a balance of $15,000. You are telling me that you didn't make this purchase?"

"Yes, as a matter of fact I wasn't even in the country at the time. I was in Senegal giving a charity a million dollars to help aide children with financial needs."

"Well sir, have you made any purchases prior to leaving the country that may verify this purchase."

"No"

"Well sir, our investigation usually takes a month to properly probe around and get facts together. I'll try to go ahead and speed up this process."

"How will I know how or when to contact you? Can I have your name and direct extension number or any contact number so that I can call to speak specifically with you?"

"Yes"

"I'm going to contact you in two weeks so that I know something is being done."

"That's not a problem sir. In the meantime, you probably want to call all your credit card companies and put a hold on any credit cards you have. There is a big possibility that you need to contact all credit bureau's to make sure there isn't any suspicious activity going on."

"Do you have their phone numbers?"

"Yes, for Experian, Trans union, and Equifax give me just a second."

Oh my God, if this is another trial that I have to learn something out of it, Lord please let this go by smoothly and easily.

What kind of shit is this? This will look bad on my record. I am an accountant that can't keep my own shit together. I know of a Moorish group that has mastered the discharge, A4V process, and set off methods. I really need to get up with them.

Chapter 19

READING MINDS

"Ohhh Baby can you come over tonight?" LaKesha asked.

"Baby what's wrong? Are you okay? You don't sound so well." I asked

Clearing her voice, "I just need you to come over after work; do you have time for me?"

"Yes of course, now you know baby I got you . . . anything you need from the store?

"Yessssss."

"Okay what is it?"

"I don't know if you want to go get it for me . . . ."

"Please don't tell me you want me to go to the store and by some pads and Midol?"

In a quoi voice, "Well baby, my period came on kind of hard this time . . . I don't have the strength to even get up out of the bed . . . I had to call the week off a work . . ."

"Ummm . . . and where are your home girls???"

"Their at work . . . Please go to the store for me . . ."

"Hummm." Damn here we go.

"Well you know what, It's okay . . . don't worry about it . . . . I'll take care of it!!!"

"I have to come after work sweetie . . ."

"Don't worry about it I got it . . ." Click

Man . . . She must be on the edge . . . I tell you the worst thing about women when they are on their periods is this constant mood swing. Sometimes they feel like a nut and sometimes they don't . . . . When you don't get exactly what they want they go in the rage and have you looking like a dummy with a cone on your head . . . LaKesha is a little to grown to not to have a stash . . . She's just playing trying to see if I would accommodate her in her time of need.

I just rather a woman would depend on themselves for certain things . . . I'll pay the bill do whatever I have to do . . . but when I start seeing Monistat 7, pads all slung over in the bathroom closet, pink lace, and just shit all everywhere it's not supposed to be.. ugghhhh . . . . I know a woman had to keep up here hygiene but damn do I have to do everything . . . .

After 5 hours of crying snot and tears.

I cannot believe Ron . . . I go everywhere he needs me to go when he assskkkss me any fucking thing in the world . . . I ask for one simple thing and he tells me NO! Let me call Liz . . . .

"You have reached the right number but unfortunately at the wrong time, please leave a message and I'll get back to you as soon as I can, Be Blessed."

Liz this is LaKesha. Girl you will not believe this shit this mother fucker did. Call me as soon as you get this message . . .

5 minutes later

"LaKesha, girl what's going on?"

Girl you will not believe I called Ron to go and get me some pads and some Midol, before I even get the words out girl he just brushes me all the way off about it..

"No he didn't"

"Yeah, girl . . ."

"I could have gone and got if for you . . . I'm off today . . ."

"Girl it's not even that . . . it's just the principle of the thing . . . I'm giving him all this quality time and my ass and he can't come off his high horse and get me one thing . . . That's why I don't like dating guys that have more money than me . . . They act like they are the gift to the world and don't have to answer to no one . . . Cocky Ass Mother Fucker . . . He can go the fuck to hell!!!"

"Girl just calm down . . . most guys are not into all of that stuff . . . that's why you have girl friends . . ."

RING RING RING

"Girl someone is at my door . . . ."

"Liz all in the cool-aid, "who is it?'"

"Girl I don't know?"

KNOCK KNOCK KNOCK

"Whispering, Girl its Ron . . . I'm going to hide in the closet."

"Answer the door!" Liz demanded . . .

"No that mother fucker can take that shit somewhere else . . ."

"Girl he might have what you need . . ."

"So the fuck what . . . . He done pissed me off for today . . . he can stand there all he wants . . . his Black ass is not coming in here . . . ."

"Girl you a mess, now you know there's always a reaction for your actions, let me not go down memory lane on you."

"No he's the mess!" Looking down at her phone . . . **CALL WAITING** Ron . . . . Text "I'm at the door."

"And I'm not available mother fucker . . ."

"Poor Ron?"

"Poor me . . . I can't believe him . . . I'll call you back . . . I need a glass of wine to calm my nerves . . ."

A week later, LaKesha sitting at her desk handling the new marketing campaign coming up for the new quarter.

"Miss LaKesha we have a delivery at the front desk for you. Do you want us to bring it to you or you can come pick it up?" The security guard asked in his very flirtatious voice.

"Oh are they from you?"

"No it's from someone; you know I'm not supposed to read personal messages."

"What is it?"

"A box and a dozen yellow roses from Flowers.com, special delivery for the Queen . . . ha ha."

"You can send it in." I cannot leave my desk; I have entirely too much paper work to do. This Latino brother came through the door with his polo sport colon just changing the aroma in my office.

"Baby, please forgive me. You mean more that this world to me. Can we meet at J. Alexander's for dinner tonight?" He said with a sad face.

"Hummm they do pay you well."

"Here's your flowers Madame, someone really loves you . . ."

"What's love got to do with it?" My eyes cut him so quick that he nearly tripped over himself trying to get out the door. I have to call Liz hum, No she'll try to defend his ass. Let me call Shartel.

"Shartel Speaking"

"Are you free to talk?" with hope and anticipation. Shartel has this nice ear to hear. She always listens to me.

"Yes, I'm on my break"

"Girl you will not believe what Mr. Jenkins sent me?"

"What? Is it an engagement ring?"

As I went to open the yellow and green little box, "No, A Tiffany's Charm set."

"Charm bracelet, earrings and necklace?"

"Yes girl, a handsome delivery man begging me for forgiveness. I should have asked for his number in spite."

"You need to quit. Ya'll been together going on a year, Shartel sarcastically said.

"Hum whatever"

"At least he has not given up on you yet because I know you and that trifling shit that you pull on some of those men you have been dating, you make a brother not even want to look at another sister in the face."

"Girl did I tell you that he didn't want to go to the store and pick up my emergencies?"

"Your emergencies? Here you go with these new phrases"

"Yeah you know when the moon sends a vibration to your pituitary?"

"What?"

"You know when the moon sends a vibration to your pituitary that helps to influences hormonal balance?"

"Girl, see you are all over my head with that mess, your mom sure have home schooled you far too hard not to become a surgeon."

"Ha ha, girl had me dissecting frogs and cats in the back yard, everyone is not made to bed cutting open people. That first site of seeing a cadaver in college was a wrap for me."

"Oh do I remember when you tortured me running me all down the street with frog legs."

"Ha, ha, ha . . . those where your gift you remember how you use to always have those wet dreams, so a pair of frog pants would make you fit right in with your body excrement's."

"Ha, ha, hell that shit ain't funny! I told you that my uncle was molesting me."

"Yeah girl but we handled him like we were Charlie's Angels and had his ass arrested."

"Yeah that shit was funny, he started asking me for forgiveness and we both whipped the shit out of him when the police went to file a report."

"Those were the day's honey but yeah it was that time of the month breaking it down in layman's terms. The moon sends a vibration to your hypothalamus, which sends another vibration or frequency whatever you have it, down to your uterus and if you have not conceived it crushes the egg inside you.

"Say what?"

"Yeah and you know when you think of your cycle, get that everything revolves around the lunar "moon" cycle. It's actually three days before your cycle comes on that the process has begun. Your body just goes through those hormonal shifts before and bleeds in the cleansing process."

"I know that's right because right before I start having mine girl I have this freakiness alarm come on before and two days after my period. It's like I need to fuck every man with two legs walking."

"That's that animal nature in you, Mother Nature is trying to reproduce and she does not care who you reproduce with. That's why you have to have spirit control over your flesh."

"Animal nature, mother nature, whatever you want to call it, my kick stands come up and I have to shake a leg."

"Girl you're a mess . . . lol. But, this fool did not even want to go and get me some Midol's or some pads. Hell he could have stopped by Chucks Grocery Store and picked me up some alkaline water and magnesium caps just to ease the pain. But no he didn't." I had to gather up me a crew that was for me.

"Sounds like make up sex to me!" Shartel said in her freaky voice.

"After being with . . . . You know Lloyd Hawkins; Ron will have to work harder than that, that shit will not work here.

"Girl thanks for the PMS Medical dissertation but I have to prepare these files for my attorney's hearing coming up.

Chapter 20

Relaxing in the Arms of Love

Miss LaKesha this is Kathy Craig calling from the Human Resources Department. We need you to come into the Human Resources Department before your scheduled shift."

"Okay am I in trouble or something?"

"I can't discuss anything over the phone with you at this time. So when you get to the Human Resource department, just have them page me so that I can speak with you.

"Okay." Oh Shit. They are going to fire me. NooooNooooNooo not supposed to think about that I do not need to just start forming all these assumptions because they did not tell me anything yet.

OMG thoughts just began to run around my mind. After 10 years of all my hard work they are firing me. I come to work on time sometimes 10 to 15 minutes early and I stay after hours making sure that all things are caught up.

I just can't believe this shit. I may need a drink after this one. Why me O God, Why me . . . I should just go in that mother fucker and start throwing over chairs and tables and throwing shit everywhere. No don't need to do that the police department is right on 22nd avenue and how all these police are on every corner they will have me in Orient Road in a split second. Fuck, I can't do that I still have to find another job.

These slimy bitches, I was just talking to Kathy and them the other day and she could have given me a heads up or something. That's what I thought friends were for. Shit I had to create my own job inside the company just so that they wouldn't fire me years ago. I know I should have seen this coming I was the only Black female next to Arnold Green a Black brother in Technical Support. We all transferred into Tampa so that we could restart this division and regardless of what people think this is still the south and some of these folks are still stuck mentally in those good ol days . . . when those good 'ol people only look out after each other.. and then again everyone no matter what race people are stabbing each other in the back or undermining you just so that they can keep their pay check to paycheck bouje life style.

Well I have $100,000.00 in my savings and I have some much stock in this company along with my IRA and bonds that my parents and grandparents left me . . . . so I really don't have to stress about anything. I'm cashing all my shit the Fuck in . . . Fuck that . . . they will experience a huge hit since I have 20 percent in the marketing department. Just stop . . . I really don't know what's going to happen so let me just stop and take a shower and put on my best sexy dress because I might just have to stop in to Bernini's and have a few drinks.

Hummmm what should I do . . . . Walking into my bathroom . . . so upset and confused. I really do not know what to do . . . So discussed with myself I can't even look at myself in the mirror . . . Should I take a shower or soak it out with a bubble bath. Shit a shower is quick and to the point.

Humm let me handle this and be done. I jumped into the mirror and affirmed to myself this is just my transition, God has something better for me; it's going to be alright. I still have my right mind, body, and soul. God has always provided and will provide all my needs. I accept and deserve the best in my life. I am a money magnet and I am money. Money I am your honey and you love me. Thank God for Reverend Ike. Lord, just help a sister in need. What am I going to do? I'm to overly qualified to get a job. I had already been searching around and I may just have to go back to Philly just so that I can have something descent to work with. But I just found the man of my dreams and I really don't want to lose out on that. The only man that I know has my back on anything. Sheeeesshhhh what am I worrying about Ron has never shown any qualities of leaving me. But men do get kind of edgy when they find out you are going to be depending on them. But Ron comes from a great family; I don't have anything to worry about.

I need to shake myself... Feels like I'm having an anxiety attack. My hands started to shake then my legs . . . I nearly tripped over myself making my way to the door. I should just go and get some of those muscle relaxers Shartel gave. All this anxiety is nothing but fear of the unknown. I need to just take 10 deep breaths my life still goes on after this. I think I can convince Ron to take me to the Bahamas for the weekend he's always talking about getting out of the country for the week. All these cheap cruises for $200 and I do have my passport. Let me just get this over with.

Arriving at the job . . ."Thanks for stopping by." Kathy said in this warming voice.

"Your welcome, so what's going on?"

"Well just give me a second; I will have a representative come in from security."

As the door opened I already knew what the deal was. Kevin the flirt from security could not believe it was me when he came in.

"Well Miss . . . . Due to the unforeseen events the company is letting go of some of our best employees. The company is downsizing and has added a new company just to survive in the ongoing changes in the economy and expanding into more global economies. Most of the company has been moved to India.

"Oh, NO, I can't believe this!" As I tried to hold back my tears.

"Yes, it's unfortunate but that's what s going on. We already packed your belonging from your desk and its waiting for you outside in the front."

"Oh, no"

"We ask that you don't make a scene and just remove yourself from the premises. Kevin will escort you out." Kathy went to shake my hand.

"But what about my staff?" I just looked at her and slid my hand so fast through her palm she couldn't even get a grip.

"They have been taken care of."

"But Kathy!!! Why couldn't you have told me what was going on ahead of time. I thought you had my back, I thought you were my friend?

"I will always be your friends but this is just my job and I 'm just doing what I have to do, you know we all have to pay the bills and especially the mortgage or rent."

"But." Bitch . . . This shit ain't funny. I turned my back and headed out the door.

"Sorry about this one sweat heart they didn't even tell me what they were doing today. I know you'll do okay, those good looks of yours can land you in another jobs faster than I can blink my eye." Kevin said as he escorted me to the door.

"Can you get this for me? I was not prepared to be carrying a heavy box like this one."

"Why sure anything for the prettiest woman I have ever seen coming through the doors." Kevin said as he grabbed my things and walked me to my car.

"Just don't put your heart into this company or any company unless it's your own honey."

"Well, my family is straight from Kingston Jamaica and you know I have to other jobs besides this. Have to make sure my family is taken care of. Be strong sister gal. God will provide."

"Thanks Kevin, nice meeting you."

"Don't be a stranger, just hit me up at the Caribbean Club on Saturday's, I'm a Dj"

"Alright, that's what I'm talking about, have a nice day."

"You do the same and keep your head up."

"Most definitely will."

Company Email

Effective Immediately LaKesha . . . . Is no longer working at Verizon

Okay LaKesha you have to pull your shit together. I just could not hold back the tears. My heart was broken. Why did they have to let me go? I gave that company my heart all my hard work . . . all my time. I missed so many family events even times that I could have chilled with my Uncle Freddy-Bear before he passed. They can go to HELL. I don't need them, they need me. Tears just coming down so fast I had to slow down . . . I need a fucking drink . . . I turned down 56th street turned down Martin Luther King Blvd just to keep away from people looking at me. I arrived at Bernini's dried my tears took a few breaths and took a table in the outside patio away from the corner.

"How can I help you mama?"

"I need a shot of Hennessy and a bottle of Remy for starters."

"Ruff day?" The waitress asked

"Let's not even go there with that."

"Here's your menu, I will give you a few minutes to order."

"Hummmm . . ." That carpaccino looks tasty . . . no no will have a hard time digesting that beef with IBS . . . that shrimp scampi . . . no cooked that last night . . . okay the egg plant will work and pistachio grouper."

Just as I was getting to the end of my entrée . . . Reggie Hawkins walked by. I could not believe It I had not seen him in a while.

"What's up Kesha?" He asked.

"Nothing much, how is life treating you?" I asked.

"Well, I tell you I meet this beautiful woman and I think I'm going to marry her?"

"You, Reggie Hawkins are getting married? I know you had to have at least 2 or 3 women on the side?"

"Yeah they okay with it. Shot. If they are not down with me making my main lady my wifey, they can hit the door you know another chicken head will suffice."

I started slowly to get another panic attack. "Oh really, 4 years since the last time I saw you and nothing has changed." Looking just like his brother. I began taking deep breaths to calm myself down. After finally getting a restraining order against his brother after 2 years of beatings and being humiliated in front of my friends, enough was enough. I had a relapse in the middle of the day along with getting fired I need to hit another glass of Remy."

"Mind if I join you."

"No come on sit."

"You alright, Kesh, you looking a little shaky?"

"Yeah, I'm alright just had to stop here and get me a drink."

"Umm, I'm sorry to hear about what my brother did to you, you know growing up that's all we saw our Pops do to our mother. Things could be okay and then the next minute the beatings would start," his head dropped.

I will not regret the day that I met Lloyd Hawkins, but this I do know I'm a better woman without him around, "Man o man."

"You are such a beautiful woman I would have never put my hands on you. Lloyd jealous ass."

"Just got fired, I know you wouldn't have, I'm okay now. I have someone in my life as well. He's treating me really well."

"My empathy to you on that one, it's getting hard out here these days everyone is having it hard with this economy like it is. I see that you are being loved, from the size of that Yellow Diamond on your finger, very well," he said motioning for my hand blinking really hard.

"Yeah, he loves me." I began to gloat.

"So what brings you to Bernini's of Ybor in the middle of the day?"

"Well it's one of my favorite restaurants . . . Had to come here since J'Alexander's is so far and Cephas Restaurant is under renovation. Along with the fact that I need a drink right now!"

"Hey, I can understand that. Don't mess with an Alichi's drink. Gotts to get it in."

"Shoot after I did that liver detox with all that sodium and olive oil . . . this is my very 1st few drinks after 3 months."

"Ughhh . . . you and all that damn detoxing. Your body should be clean as a whip. You still on that every three month bit of detoxing?" Blinking his eyes and laughing, "I can see clearly now that that Alch was gone . . . ha haha."

"I have to stay clean. It's far too many poisoning in the air, food, and water these days. Don't just consume it because they say it's good for you. Could be the worst thing you bring into your body chemistry."

"Is your famous Reiki Master Healer still around?"

"Who, can't think of his name right now hum it's been so long, yeah Alim Bey, yeah he still doing his thing. Ha ha ha . . . now he's out in North Carolina now, I'll tell him that you asked about him."

"You know he must be doing it big if he has his own company right about now."

"Yeah . . . . Thanks for reminding me I'm going to have to call him later on. I need a healing session. This job done laid me off and ummm . . ."

"Nawwwhhh not . . . you just another dedicated sister to helping the man get where he needs to get. At the end of the deal you're useless and used up."

"Yea, you can say whatever but I have ventures going on and I still have to pay those bills and put food in my mouth. How you doing?" My momma sure didn't' raise any fool. I may have ridden the short bus when it comes to relationships with some of these brothers down south but going through all that shit with your brother and others using me for my money . . . ENOUGH IS ENOUGH . . . yeah they gave me a few douses but this man is the one. I feel it in my heart."

"Ha but you know us southern gentlemen give the best kind of love and everyone is not the same. So don't throw me in the bottom of the barrel with all those other crabs."

"So true, thanks for introducing me into metaphysics. I would have never been able to regroup from this or the other challenges that I had to face."

"No problem Goddess I know I had to get myself back into place after all those years of domestic violence and all the struggling my family had us going through . . . Then on top of that I was going to church and seeing the same ones in the pulpit or in the choir right at the Casino's or switching streets down Nebraska or mysteriously popping up at the strip club. I couldn't but let you know the truth. That Willie Lynch Chip and all this programming going on for so many years it's just hard for someone to remove themselves it's like the night of the living dead out here. Most of my peoples out here are suffering and they don't have to. How we come from building Pyramids to the projects . . . from sailing the seas to being too scared to even jump in the water."

"Umm. Now you know that's right." He reminded me of Brother Dawud, but I don't even think he even met him. More eccentric but his energy he was giving shook me up. But at the end of the day he was right. I had given all my time to a company that turned around and just told me to kiss their ass. But what to do now . . . that was my life . . . I loved creating things. Tears began to form at my eyes I guess that mixture of Hennessy and Remy was getting to me . . . and I just let go . . .

"Kesha, girl it's alright, it will be okay. Can I get some napkins?" When Reggie put his arms around me, I thought it was Ron and tears just came running. I couldn't hold it Reggie's Energy just was so healing. I didn't care.

"Just breathe honey, take some deep breaths it will be okay. It's not what happens to you it's how you respond."

The waiter ran from inside with napkins, "Is she alright?"

"Yeah, she'll be okay."

"Baby, just giving you a call looks like I just saw someone that looks just like you. Give me a call when you get this message." Riding through the heart of Tampa you are susceptible to see just anyone out of the wood works that you haven't seen before. Here I'm riding through Ybor City on my way home and I see Jayla's new boyfriend hugged up on someone that looked like my woman. Humm I'm not going to escalate but I will be making this u-turn around this corner and make sure this is not her. Just as I went to park the car a police rolled right up behind me. I'll talk with her later. She must be on her lunch break doing business and I know I'm working on my anger management.

Chapter 21

Setting Matters Straight

Let me get myself together before I go into this house. I can't believe this girl all this time I've been doing my best to please her taking her places taking time out of my schedule . . . It took me to drive down Ybor City in the middle of the day to find her in the arms of another man. How long has this shit been going on? Is she fucking him to? No No No I'm just over exaggerating. I have a good girl she wouldn't do no shit like that I can trust her . . .

A few deep breaths before I get out this truck. I do not need to make any drastic moves with this because if I even come close to her and someone see's us arguing here comes Tampa Police to throw a mother fucker in jail. Fuck, how should I do this, since I have the key to the crib I should just go ahead and walk in. No have to be a man about this because I'm too heated at the moment. Let me just go ahead and call to see where she's at . . .

RING RING RING

RING RING RING

RING RING RING

"You have reached LaKesha's voicemail unfortunately I'm unavailable please leave a message after the tone and I'll get back with you as soon as possible . . . ."

Taking a deep breath, "Kesha this is Ron, I've been calling you all day to see what's going on give me a call back."

RING RING RING

RING RING RING

RING RING RING

Let me call again . . . "I'll see you at your place!"

Shaking myself right before I left the elevator arriving at her door. I went to jiggle the keys in the door. Placing my ear towards the door I heard Sade playing. My anger had peaked, let me breath slow it's not what I think it is . . .

Walking through the door, I saw LaKesha laying down in a man's arms on her ataman, "What the FUCK is going on" This kat looked at me shook, LaKesha out of her sleep.. "Kesha wake up."

Hearing this loud voice she turned and looked at me, "Kesha what the fuck is going on here?"

Her eyes half way open, "Nothing, what do you mean what's going on?"

"What the FUCK are you doing with this kat?"

"Nothing"

"Is there a problem?" He asked me with a smirk on his face.

"Yeah mother fucker there is a problem, Kesha I have been calling you all day trying to figure out what's going on with you and all you have to say is nothing?"

"Reggie, you might want to leave."

"Yeah you need to get the fuck out of here!!!."

"If you have a problem with me playa we can handle it."

This 5'5 mother fucker is going to size me up, "Hommie I'm not looking for any problems. So you just need to carry your ass out the door . . . ."

He ran up on me . . . wrong mistake, "Ron, leave him alone, he didn't do anything to you!" LaKesha said, running in between us.

"Kesha get back!" You're a mother fucking joke give up home you ain't going to win. What the fuck you think you going to roll in here and think you can run this show? I asked your ass to leave"

LaKesha all frantic, "What the fuck you doing Ron?

"Get the fuck out of this house!" I had dude in a headlock against the ground. He still had anger in him and was trying to get free.

"Kesha get back!"

LaKesha crying, "Ron will you stop he's just a friend."

"A friend my ass, just give up hommie and leave."

"Ron Stop!"

"What the fuck Kesha I have been calling you all day and here you are with this mother fucker . . . and he has the nerve to rush on me. Fuck that just give up!"

"What are you doing?"

"So this is what you do to me, I've been spending all my time and spending all my money. This is what I fucking get for opening my heart . . . I can't believe this . . . Fuck it with all this time I have put in . . . Mother fucker I'm going to let you go don't try anything stupid. IT'S OVER!!!"

Getting up from the floor . . . this mother fucker still charges at me, thump and he was on the floor. "Told you mother fucker, **LOOK LIKE YOU GOT KNOCKED THE FUCK OUT!"**

LaKesha running to me than running to get this kat up off the floor, "Ron it's not what it looks like . . . We can work this out . . ."

"What the fuck . . . Am I suppose to believe some bullshit like that you sitting up here with your night gown on and laying in the arms of this fool**, GET THE FUCK OUT OF HERE!!! IT'S OVER!!!**" I have dealt with your attitude. I forgave how you were treating me and you still came nagging at me talking about you are going to change how you treat me. And how you so different from other women . . . . Please this is it find some feminized man to stroke your fucking ego!!! **YOUR LOTUS BLOSSUM IS REALLY STINKING RIGHT NOW!!!**"

Slamming the door making my exit to my truck . . . Tampa Police pulled in just as I was pulling out . . . .

Chapter 22

RING RING RING

"Heyyyyy my one and only and beautiful Momma."

"Ronnnnn, where's Julian? Don't let my baby get hurt!!!!" She struggled to get out.

"Momma, what's wrong?" I asked.

"Ronnnnnn!!!!"

"What's happening Momma?

"Helpp Ronnn!!!"

"Where are you on the floor, I can't get up. Please help me Ron! She said.

"Ohhhh Shitt!!!" I picked up my phone dialing 911, "I have an emergency my Momma has collapse she lives at 1901 E. Alvin St. I'm on my way there right now. There is a key under the flower pot for the front door. She needs to be transported to St. Joseph's Hospital they have all her information in their system."

Speeding through traffic, arriving at Momma's house there was no fire truck and ambulance were at the residence there was a police officer on the scene and was watching the house.

"Excuse me officer, where you here when the ambulance came?" I asked pacing and out of breath.

"Why yes, they have taken the lady to the hospital as her son requested."

"Ohh thanks, I have run."

Rushing to the hospital it starts to rain. **GOD DAMN**. I need to be there for Momma. What the fuck am I going to do? Hell, I need to call Aunty Geraldine since she doesn't do a thing with her time each and every day.

"Aunty tell everyone I'm rushing my Momma to St. Joseph's Hospital I'm on my way, I was at her house and I'm on my way. I can't make it in time its 5 o'clock traffic and it's pouring down rain. It may take me two hours to get there."

"Okay sweetie I'm on my way," Aunty Geraldine stated.

Aunty Geraldine jumping out of her car and ran to stand alongside Amber. Nurses assist Amber into the facility. Amber's eyes rolling back and forth, like she lost consciousness.

1 HOUR PASSES

Everyone arrives at the hospital. The Doctors said Momma just had a minor break down. That she will be okay. She just needs to rest. Okay. Momma sat resting in her hospital bed, sleeping like a baby.

That damn Julian, his ass got himself into some deep shit and sent Momma into a panic attack that mothafucka can die. For all I care right now.

"Ron don't say that," Jaya said.

"I say what the hell I want to say and that mother fucker has crossed the lines. Common sense would have told him not to come to Momma with that shit."

"Well you don't talk to him Ron," Aunty Geraldine said.

"And you know I don't have time for foolishness," Aunty Louise said.

"Momma's trying to gain her health," I said

Chapter 23

Unexpected Visit

Sitting back looking at the dry erase board in the middle of the dining room filled with 100 Black Men of Tampa, I had took a deep breath. It was the middle of our business meeting for the quarter. Anytime you start talking about numbers people tend to doze off. It's great that our President tries to spice things up every now and then because right about now my body will shut down at the hint of silence. There were hors devours on the table along with some drinks. You know just to keep the brothers stomachs going because there was no way I was going to table feed them. Shoot if they want some plate food they best bring their own or have something prepared for them at home.

It hit about 9o'clock the meeting was a little too out drawn but it was okay because we hit a lot of topics.

"There is an all-time high of single parents living and these young boys really don't have anyone to look after them." A new topic the President stated as if it was an emergency. I really don't even have time to nurture a young man. So, I just simply sponsor for a member to go along with mentoring.

SQUEEEKKK SQUEEEK SQUUUEEEK "Another topic of discussion having a 1,000 man march each year. It will be a celebration and to show black women and children that real men do exist."

I know it was time for this meeting to adjourn because I had to wake right back up at 6:30AM in the morning for my workout.

RING RING RING

Everyone looked at the door and turned their heads towards me.

"I'll get it."

Looking at the TV screen by the door to see who it was, Oh Shit. LaKesha was at the door in a trench coat. This girl is off the chain popping up here without telling me.

Cracking the door open giving her the cold shoulder since we did separate, "I'm in a meeting."

"So"

"It's too many men in here and you know that I don't want everyone in my business."

"So, what are you trying to tell me?"

"Come back in half an hour."

"Okay don't keep me waiting . . . . or I will have to come in and disrupt everything."

After leaving the room I didn't want to explain what had happened but the meeting was headed toward an end. I gave my president the eye.

"Well gentleman it was fun discussing all the objectives that we have but the time is right for us all to return back home."

"You ain't lying I have to wake up at 5 am to do my run on the beach and it's already my bed time," one member made the point to mention.

Everyone else had agreed.

RING RING RING

1/2 HOUR HAD PASSED

It was LaKesha. Boy I just can't wait to see what she had hiding behind that trench coat. All is fair in love and war! She walked through the door and gave me a kiss as she led me to the sofa. "I have something awaiting you upstairs"

"Like what?" I questioned.

"Now what was up with you that you that I found you in the arms of another man?"

Gently touching my face with her hand, "I was under so much pressure honey. I had just lost my job and it hit me really hard."

"So why didn't you come to me about it, you could have called me or something to let me at least know."

"I didn't want to disturb you with my problems."

"How the hell you didn't want to disturb me, hell you call me about picking up tampons and I came and dropped them off but you still act like there is something wrong with this relationship. Just because I don't always come when you need or pick up the phone does not me mean I'm too busy for you. From here on out don't do that shit anymore! Are you going to give me you all or are we going to have to settle this right now?"

"Baby all I want is you. Reggie is like a brother to me."

"Oh really, well Reggie needs to know when to step to the side when we are having a conversation. What's going on with us has nothing to do with anyone else."

"Okay honey. I want you to show more affection and attention to me."

"That's not a problem all you have to do is let me know. Your actions are sure telling me something totally different. I didn't come into this relationship trying to be with another man. Did you fuck him?"

Looking at me with disdain and not saying a word.

"Did you fuck him?"

"No Ron, like I said Reggie is like a brother and just friends. I use to be with his brother and let's just say things didn't last. Reggie and I still remained close."

Reaching the room LaKesha started right at my chest with her soft lips touching against my body. Never had I had a woman start there usually it would be around my ears or a nice warm welcoming French kiss. She had unzipped my pants and threw me on to the bed. This girl almost had the strength of a man. I looked at my white and blue checkered boxers sliding half way off my ass. She started moving her hands down them. My dick was already hard. She then slipped them down half way towards my knees. Next thing I know she took me into her mouth . . . . Damn. Her tongue just swirled around my chest nipples at lightning speeds that my dick began to thump even more. Shit this some good shit I have rolled on.

The summer season looked like the best opportunity to vacation. I should say the beginning and middle. Once you hit the tail end of a hot Florida summer it seems as though the 4 winds of the Bermuda Triangle go into affect one minute it floods in Tennessee, next second there's a fire or earth quake in California, a tornado in Kansas the hurricane season for Florida, Gulf Coast Area and North east bordering states. I'm just so surprised at this point that the Gulf Stream didn't reverse but I'm just simply thinking. I just need to go ahead and take LaKesha on a little cruise something close in the area just so that if anything goes down in the office I can quickly come back then again I have my vacation time planned to take a tour of Kemet (Egypt) with Bro. Kwesi and the next two weeks catch another trip through Asia on a trip to find the traces of the remnants of Blacks with Dr. Runoko Rashidi.

Looking through the internet boom "Starlight Ship cruises, special going for the summer $35 each person sounds like a plan.

"Kesha are you free this weekend?"

"You already know, I have a full plate."

"Well don't you want to see me?"

"Humm . . . all depends on what you need a hug or something?"

"So I guess you too busy for me."

"Sweetie it's the middle of the quarter and I'm preparing for strategies so that I can prepare a few marketing proposal's for this new plan.

"Ummm . . . So how long are you going to be **MISS INDEPENDENT** and when are you going to allow me to be the man for you?"

"Now honey you know I work and go all over and above for this 9-5 career. I'm already barely making it thanks to God . . . there's no one giving hand out these days. Having on this body suite sometimes creates the environment that I have to work 3-5 times harder than the average person."

"I heard that, but baby if you are talking about making a home you have to make an adjustment."

"Yeah, yeah, yeah someone told me love has to be maintained and love has to recuperated the thing is maintenance and reciprocation don't pay my bills, what does love have to do with it?"

"Plenty . . . YOU!!!

Chapter 24

Arriving at Grandma's House

"Now baby put your bullet proof vest on my aunties are going to hit you hard and watch out for Uncle Al he'll probably try to sweet talk you.

"Greetings everyone I have brought my girlfriend LaKesha here today with me. So please throw down your knives and welcome her in.

Aunty Geraldine and Louise looked at each other and simultaneously said, "My . . . My!!"

"Well come on in honey," Grandma said as she made her way around the table.

This Sunday the family had thought of doing. "Do your Dance a Thon" and we all wanted to see who could do their best dance. We opted out of the cheering like it was Show Time at the Apollo and changed it around to the panel of judges like American Idol, nothing but an updated Apollo. Who make the perfect mode of judging was none other than Grandma, Aunty Geraldine, and Aunty Louise.

Uncle Al came through the center of the room looking like James Brown decked down with some super tight black pants, a split open red shirt covered in jewelry dangling everywhere as if he was Rick James.. Showing his entire chest, with a black coat and red cape, he walked to the center of the mock stage and when I tell you he walked in blowing kisses at all the women . . . . they couldn't help but blush and laugh . . .

"Hot Damn that damn Al has done it again," Aunty Louise raspy voice laughed at an extremely high pitch.

Uncle Al couldn't help but give a little chuckle himself. It was as if we were stuck in a time machine. As he pulled the mic toward him he gave us 2 minutes of this a man's world . . .

"Bobby hit me one, two, three, and four . . ." He pulled off the cape and started jerking from one end of the stage to the other . . .

"Get on up, got to stay on the scene like a sex, machine that's the way I like it, that's the way that it is . . . and topped it off with a moon walk . . . followed by, "Baby baby baby . . . I got that feeling . . . ."

All the judges gave him a perfect 10.

"Some people just can't let James go . . . lawd have mercy . . . and we all do know that Al is a sex machine . . . ha ha," Grandma said.

"I couldn't help myself but that performance was like having a menopausal hot flash all over again. Somebody please give me a fan before I faint." Aunty Geraldine said fanning herself moving from side to side in her chair.

In a loud pitch from out of nowhere, "Geraldine, don't let me have to call 9 1 1, Momma said." Everyone was just hysterical. Even Uncle Al was bent over laughing.

"Sweat running down the sides of his face ha ha ha," Grandma laughing hysterically. And to add insult to injury, two cousins of ours came with fans and his red cape to place back over Uncle.

"Thank you, thank you, I just want to give a shot out to Lucille, who was the best woman that I ever had in my life God rest her soul," Uncle said in this soft voice a tear fell from the side of his face.

"Awwhhhh, Al it's okay," Momma ran and hugged Uncle Al it was like he had an emotional breakdown during the performance.

I was just so shocked I should have brought her around a little sooner. There was no fight's everyone was on their best behavior and was really excited for me. Last but not least this was my moment. I went into the dressing room; I had Momma put in my cd . . . "Just keep it in the closet!" Michael Jackson's voice aired the room, my signal to come out the door. I had my white shirt, tight black jeans, white socks and penny loafers. As I left the wall, I tilted my hat as Billy Jean aired, I made my way to the stage everyone's mouth was completely open the next second I was on top of the stage, "I want to love you Pretty Young Thing," as I gestured towards LaKesha. Her head just went down she was smiling from t to t.

From the corner of my eye I saw Julian come into the room give Mom a kiss, looked at me and nodded his head and went back out the door. You talk about a mood crusher. Momma looked right into my eyes smiled and lipped synced, "don't worry baby your Momma is very proud of you," and blew a kiss to me. I tell you the charisma, mannerism, and sultry words coming from Momma always seemed to warm my heart even at the most difficulties times. I always wanted my brother to be a brother and share in whatever I did. But by his actions on this day, just put the nail in the coffin. There was no need for me to keep compromising myself and forgiving this Fucker after almost damaging my credit, stealing my identity, and my money. Many people can say God give me strength but in the end, but if it walks like an ASS, looks like an ASS, and act's like an ASS, then for Pete's sake **IT'S A DAMN JACK ASS**, literally and everywhere it moves the shit just stinks.

"**Baby so when am** I going to have me some grandkids?" Momma was on the phone at her usually midnight clock work."

"Well mom we haven't discussed all that yet."

"She's a nice looking girl, easy on the eyes."

"Yeah Momma, when I first seen her making her way through the crowd."

Interjecting with an attitude, "At a club?"

"Yes Mamme, I know you told me a girl in the club is only worth a dub."

"Hummm," Momma giving off this sigh of don't let your shit hit the fan.

"But Mom it's not even like that, LaKesha is a different girl. You told me how to look for a good wife Mom. The majority of the qualities that you have, I want my woman to have and LaKesha has a great career in marketing and she's selling Mary Kay on the side. You really don't have to worry about her family has left her with quite a bit of money."

"Seems like you did your footwork on finding out about her but anything that walks with two legs and pussy between it, is a different girl, Ron!"

"Yes, we both had background checks, blood tests on each other already Mom. We also wanted to make sure that if had any imbalances in our body's to get them corrected before we start having children. We did agree to have healthy children. Which included me and her both changing our eating habits."

"Well, I just don't want your heart being broken again, Honey, it's like you fall hard for these girls and they fall short of my expectations of a real woman. Because baby when you are down and out, will she pick up the slack and get to work without thinking she's wearing the pants. You know some of these women these days will switch out on you like a bad transmission once things just don't go their way or hear you lost your job."

"Umm . . . Mom it will be okay. I got you; all you have to do is spend a little time with her and get to know her mom."

"Yeah, yeah, I have already made a date for us to have a sit down conversation at Candy Lowe's Tea Time, Tea Party."

"Oh Mom please don't let your friends eat her alive."

"Well honey if you got down on your knees to propose to her, a little cut or two here or there will not bother her, that's if she really loves you. You are going to marry her?"

"Ohhhh . . . interesting, why yes." I just was lost for words; LaKesha didn't mention that to me.

Within the next ten minutes of talking with Momma, Aunty Louise calls. "So I guess you and mom and other's had a talk."

"More than right to son, we just don't want someone to come and break your heart. Suga I think that it's time to have a talk about this LaKesha."

"Oh is that right, so what's your take on the matter?"

"Humm, yeah how about you come over and we have a little talk?"

"Well, I suppose to be getting with my momma earlier, but for you Aunty Louise, I'll just reschedule with Momma."

In a stern voice, "Well I don't like her, and when I say I don't like her. I DON'T LIKE HER AT ALL, alright but I really need to talk to you son."

"Okay," I'm kind of aprehensious because all the other four girls that I brought home she just didn't like them and saw right through them. For the most part they all showed their true colors. I really want to settle down and have a family now. That big 40 is knocking on my door and I can't go back and relive any of those years. It's not like I didn't try to be in a relationship.

"How about I take you to Circles tomorrow morning?"

"Okay, allow me to get my clothes together this 75 year old body does not move around like it use to. Give me to noon. Hopefully they are still serving breakfast. I just love their English waffles."

"Yes they are serving their breakfast menu at that time. Noon it is."

Chapter 25

The old folk's blues

Aunty Louise's white hair looked white as cotton as her crisp curls from her roller set was slowly loosening up. You know those old ladies don't like you combing out their curls. Their hair has to stay like that for weeks so that they can wait for the next old lady to complement them on the beauty of their hair. Her flowerily blazer hung behind her and her figure like she had not aged at all.

Grasping my hand, "Baby how have you been?"

"Great just trying to live in balance."

"So you know I have to ask you about this girl?"

"Woman?"

"A girl is not a woman until she has a child. That same woman is a mother fucker, if she doesn't spend time raising and preparing her children to meet life and the world once they leave the house. Sitting down on your ass or with your legs with your kickstands up and open will always get you what you want, most definitely it is not showing you how to be a man or woman about it either."

"Ummm," don't seem like Aunty had her coffee this morning I need to just back down and listen because there is a probability of me getting my head chopped off.

"So I had a talk with LaKesha on last Sunday. And it seems that she may be a little too much for you."

"How is that Aunty, you don't even know her?"

"Well honey she came in like she had an attitude as if her shit didn't stank."

"Now Aunty come on, most people have a demeanor but that does not mean that they are what you assume they are. You really have to get to know a person these days.

"Here's your coffee and Waffles Supreme Ma'am . . . and here is your OJ and Egg Florentine with 2 extra poached eggs . . . is there anything thing else I can assist you with?" The waitress asked.

"No that will be it for now, thanks" I stated

"Umm this is absolutely delic." Aunty said with a smile on her face.

"Well, that is your favorite dish here."

"Yes indeed, but it's made just right every time I come by." She swirled a fork with waffles and fruit with a drop of syrup just about to drop. "Well, I'll talk to you once I finish my meal, you know it's not good having emotions or feelings rise when you're eating, your food can become toxic inside your system."

"Umm . . . didn't think of that one . . . that's a good heads up."

"LaKesha is not the type to just come out and start telling you all her business. You have to warm up to her Aunty."

"If she's going to be in this family she might want to come out of her shell a little faster."

"Please don't tell me Aunty you nailed her with the 21 questions?" Oh my God. She might have just scared LaKesha.

Here eye's nearly piercing my face, "Yes honey I did, is that a problem

"No mame."

"Now if she loves you honey my strong words would be water and just roll right off her feathers."

"Ha ha . . . which is true, LaKesha loves a challenge. As thick as her skin is that drop of water will turn to vapor." Glancing off to street.

"Humm seems like you have gotten stung by the love bee, hummm see here son, and how is her family? Or where does she work? What does she do for you honey? You have to fill me in so that I can put this puzzle together."

"Humm where should I start. Aunty LaKesha is a brilliant woman that is very strong. Her parents are deceased and she has a close circle of friends that is like her sisters. She has an older brother in the New Jersey that they don't talk too much because of the age difference. She really has tough skin. It took a while before she could let me get close. Other than that Aunty she cooks, working in the marketing department as one of their top producing advertisers in her division. And last but not least she caters to all my needs."

"Ummm hum . . . well what I seen was totally opposite because one thing I know is girls like that chill you better not give in to hard."

"Well Aunty she reciprocates the love that I have for her. She introduced me into watching your favorite team the Devil Rays and went all the way out to get box seats and all."

"Go Rays, so she really does not have bad taste after all. Honey by the way your eyes are sparkling you have already fallen head over heels for her."

"I'm not going to lie. I love her Aunty. She's the woman I want to spend my life with."

"Don't be so sure honey. But since you're my boy, I'm going to tell you to put her on 3 test rule."

"Test?"

"Yes the test to see if she really loves you."

"How many tests? I don't want to scare her off."

"If her skin is as tuff as you say it is she'll survive. If not honey you might want to go somewhere else."

"Humm." I'm just worried because Aunty may have something up her sleeve. I have already tested LaKesha out. I just went along with the flow. One thing you never want to do is piss an older person off.

"I'm just saying you do what the hell you want to do. Your Aunty will always be here for you. Just don't want your heart to hurt like it did before. You had me really worried the last time honey."

"Yeah it was as if I just lost it and not eating for months. I'm stronger now Aunty. No worries I have it together."

"Alright but you take these tests and pay particular attention to how she reacts and responds. If she passes 2 of the 3 it's up to you. You can work things out with the last one."

Eager to here, "And what are these tests?"

"See honey it's not the matter of me licking her or not I could give a good God damn. But at the end of the day honey this is your happiness and love. You want someone to build a dynasty to leave a legacy. Look how your father left the accounting firm. How many accountants there are along with the trust have people had for you?"

"I can agree with that."

"Now listen up son, because you keep on interrupting me. I am going to forget the sequence of these tests."

The first test son would be to take her some where you open the door for her. On your way back to the other side of that car what she does is very important. If she sits there and does not attempt open that door you are wasting your time. If she opens that door or unlocks the doors, she's a keeper.

"Oh is that right, Grand Daddy told me that one and she passed that on the 1st date," just had to interject. I love ruffling Aunty Louise's feathers every now and then.

"Well I am his older sister," she looked and switched to the other side of the table rolling her eyes at me.

"But Aunty, why? What's does all that mean?"

"Baby, you've been around the bush to long and haven't learned a damn thang."

"Now come on Aunty, you know everyone from those times sometimes speak in riddles and I can agree that the elevator doesn't always reach certain floors. Momma always said that people don't hear have to feel and I would be that person."

"Son it means that she's not selfish. If she takes out that time to assist you, it's not all about her."

Raising my right eyebrow, with a smirk. Just to make my point to Aunty that LaKesha is one of a kind, "Well, I have done that test and she successfully passed."

"Humm"

"Yes on our first date to the movies, I took her to the movies and she changed her clothes to complement mine."

Looking me in my eyes, "The second test is play like you are sick and need her help."

"Ummm, right now I know I don't have time for that."

"Well, whenever you are in a dire need son if she sticks by your side to the end you know she's the one for you. Because a good woman is not just going to let her man go through something and not be by his side to support him. Now if your ass is in the wrong and she doesn't agree with your decision that's another thing, but you get what I'm saying."

"Got you."

"Then the next test, is to see how respectful of you around others. Because honey if a woman can't respect you when you are around your friends, family, or peers . . . she will not respect you at home . . . The entire scenario goes to Apples and Oranges. She looks like an apple bottom on the outside woman that is and on the inside she's a bitter man. Don't take it from me heard that one from Dr. Phillip Valentine and that's so true. It's alright to joke and jive every now and then but you will know when it's just plain out wrong."

"Humm, couldn't' have been said any better. Thank you so much Aunty."

"You're welcome son we all as a family have to look out even when your shit stinks we will let you know . . . but bottom line . . . I just **DO NOT LIKE** this Kieita, Kesha, La something At ALL! But it's your decision and I can only respect that!"

Chapter 26

Arriving at La Cri Bella Massage Day Spa, LaKesha and Shantel were greeted by the four receptionists. It was a nice Saturday to go and get a hair do. There were a line of women sitting and waiting to get their hair done. It was a feeling that came over the two of them that they just should go out and prepare for the evening. Looking around it was as if they had landed in the middle of Hawaii. The waterfalls that set on each side made them feel as if they were right in the midst of a tropical jungle. They were handed the keys to their lockers.

Sitting in the chair getting micro's put in her hair. LaKesha yawned.

"Girl where should we start first?"

"I don't know the sauna seems nice to go in but, I just got my hair done and I know I don't want my micros looking messy."

"Girl, that's what they have towels for. Don't act like you all brand new here. Like this is your first time being here."

"Well you know. I just like to think that way."

"Girl let's go sit in this Jacuzzi to the back away from everyone so that we can relax."

"Sounds good to me"

"Have you thought about getting a massage?"

"No but I can sure use a manicure and pedicure. My nails are chipped and they have to look fresh for tonight."

"Ummmm . . . someone must be in love. I am not going to say no names," Shantel stated as she rolled her eyes at LaKesha.

"Whatever"

"Well you been dating Ron for quite some time and this may be the day for a ring."

"Yeah it maybe but I'm not going to pressure him into doing anything. If I'm what he wants than it is what it is. Ha ha yeah that's my baby."

"Chil to find a man in Tampa with money. You know money make that pussy hollaaaa!!!"

"Girl you crazy."

"Hummm . . . Don't wait around you know how some of these women are in Tampa. They will be on the lookout especially if they see a man with money and in a relationship with someone."

"Well I'm not really that concerned with Ron. He's pretty much locked in with me."

"**OKAY OKAY OKAY . . .** have it your way. I just lost all respect for women these days. When they say bitches ain't shit, but hoes and tricks. You best keep your man close."

"Well . . . I know I must be doing something right because he already thinking about having kids with me."

"Chile and why I haven't heard about this new breaking news.

"Girl, simply because I don't know if I'm ready yet. Settling down is no joke."

"Yeah baby, but a good man is hard to find."

"I do see myself living with Ron for the rest of my life. He said that I don't have anything to worry about."

"Hell girl, if you don't follow your heart. You only have one life to live and you might as well live it up.

RING RING RING

"Speaking of the devil."

"My Jesus . . . . Give this girl some sense."

Chapter 27

THE RIGHT MAN FOR THE RIGHT JOB

"We all know that when folks fall out they fall out and they wouldn't show up around the family scene until they fall on their ass and need some form of help."

The 4th of July was always time spent with the family. It was almost like a family reunion dead in the middle of the summer. The destination was forever at Grandma's and Uncle Al had the grill going. Big mama and all the other relatives were in number and accounted for. Whoever knew how to cook either was in the kitchen or bringing a plate of their specialty piece of food to add to the forever fattening food supply?

Food was spread like a buffet. When I say everyone put their feet in the pot. They put their feet in the pot. You wonder why you gain so much weight around holiday time. It's because the food is so good that you can't help but go back for seconds or just spending seconds in pure gluttony. There are limits to everything, but around holiday time you know you best eat because that may be the first and last meal you get all year. Don't let there be some arguments between family members because you know you will not see that specialty meal until that person shows back up.

Me and my homeboys had decided to throw a 4th of July Celebration down at Channelside. It was our new yearly tradition for us as a pact. This time we all had decided to bring our women with us even if our relationships weren't in mint condition. I just knew LaKesha was going to have her own surprise waiting on me at the house after the night was over. LaKesha this girl just blows my absolute mind. I had never met someone like her before. This would be a perfect opportunity to throw an engagement to her. She just doesn't know what she has coming to her. LaKesha had gone out to Ross and made her way to Neiman Marcus to find some new clothes for the evening. She wore this elegant red dress. I had told her that I would meet her at Bernini's so that we could spend the evening there. The work load that I had today had totally set all off my plans back about an hour. To make matters worse. I had to meet a Vernon Stiles about protecting my assets and my personal life in case anything could occur. When you say security . . . you have to have all your cards backed up. It only takes one quick move and your entire life has changed. I called Jennifer to clear my schedule for the remainder of the day.

It was a beautiful day; LaKesha should be arriving here soon. I know the streets are going to be busy, so I knew we had to make it down there as quick as possible. Channelside was becoming an enormous new hot spot right next door to Ybor city. The place had grown much larger since the first time I had been down here. I thought this was just a spot for tourist and Caucasian folks. Low and behold this was the new night scene for many Blacks. Banana Joes and Splitsville attracted many by games and live music. Not to mention the IMAX movie theatre that had the softest rocking chairs. The joy of celebrating the 4th had just filled the air many people from all types of backgrounds had gathered there and there were no problems at all.

"What's up LaGwan your magic day is only one month away?" I smiled as we met in Splitsville.

"Man . . . tell me about it . . . She has me shaking in my boots already." LaGwan said as he looked and kissed Shartel on the forehead.

We chose a nice spot for us to sit at so that we could get a perfect view of fireworks. The fellas and I left the ladies sitting so that they can chat between themselves.

"Man I think this is the day?" I looked over at LaGwan.

"Ha ha be for real you know he has bumped his head if he think he's getting married," Kevin said as he looked at Kyle.

"Well I have been with this girl for over a year and she is the apple of my eye, since I put the big dick on her she's been hooked ever since." I said sternly looking at Kevin.

"Play on player just make sure you're in love," Kevin said taking a sip from his Corona.

"Well, you said that you love her, you want to please her for the rest of your life . . . so do like Otis Redding say and show her tenderness and make life happen for yourself," said Kyle.

"Word, we are all grown men here and settling down shouldn't seem so scary for us at this point. You have to follow your own heart and gut instincts because in the end it's only you that should be satisfied hell for the most part happy." LaGwan said.

Boooommmm Booooom Booooom Crack

The fireworks had started everyone was just in amusement. Ohhh shit, when should I do this? A few drops of sweat came across my brow and it felt like my heart dropped to the bottom of my stomach. All the guy's gave me the look like NOW, propose right now.

Bowing to one knee, "LaKesha I have spent one year in your presence and you have truly completed my journey. I can't see my life living without you. Will you marry me?"

"Yes, baby I will," she said as her dark brown eyes locked in mine.

Tears began rolling down her eyes all the other women that were there just started smiling and crying. Some of the fellas couldn't hold back their emotions either. Knowing that I was about to hit 36 I knew that this was the next best step in my transition to living life at my prime. The crowd around us began to cheer and said their congratulations to us as we drank the rest of the night.

As I took a walk alone with her along the edge of the strip, I just had to breathe. I was still shaking my legs nervous as hell. The feeling like I had fallen off a cliff came on me but knowing that LaKesha would be right by my side . . . . nothing else really even mattered to me.

"Baby you know I have something tucked away especially for you tonight . . . . This time at my place." She said with this huge smile across her face.

Making our way to our vehicles all of the fellas gave me their final congrats and soon after we were headed on I-275 to Bird Street. A heavy scent of smoke fumes from fireworks blew into the truck as we made our way to LaKesha's condo. There were people in the street celebrating with their own fireworks and children running around throwing fireworks at each other.

In the back of my mind the first site of me meeting LaKesha and all the times that we have spent together just took over my emotions. Those days spent at the beach playing like we were kids in a sand box. The times she popped up on me out of nowhere in a trench coat. All of her surprises had surprised me to my heart that I would actually be going through with this.

The separations that I had taken because of business had taken their toll on our relationship, but through it all me and LaKesha remained dedicated to each other. That's what I hope to believe. Shit, wait until my family gets a hold of this it's going to blow their socks off because I have not even introduced them to her since the dance off.

I just had to do the gentleman like thing and go get the door for my lady. She jumped out of the truck and landed a big kiss on my lips. Now she knows she shouldn't have done that. My emotions were at an all time high and we were ten minutes away from even reaching her door. So as I closed the door behind her my hand just had to grab on to her big juicy apple bottom.

Marriage . . . . Returning home each day just to look at LaKesha's dark eyes . . . sounded so good to me. Touching her soft dark chocolate body, man I think I can grow old with her.

Searching sporadically looking for her earrings, LaKesha had this huge panic attack. "Where are my earrings?"

"Baby what's going on?"

"Where's my bra?"

"I don't know honey."

"Well I had this already planned to go into work early today," Running to the side of the bed to give me a kiss she nearly tripped over my belt.

"Shit, you are no help right now."

"What it's okay I'm just exhausted."

Giving me this mean look, "So . . . I would have jumped for you."

"Ha ha ha lol," she know she's been working hard far too long so many years.

Her eyes cutting me, "What's so funny?"

"Baby, come here."

Sighing as she came close to the bed, "It a little late for affection, I'm already late uggh,"

A bundle of laughter in my heart holding back as I embraced her, "Baby weren't you fired?"

"Ohhhhhh **DAMN DAMN DAMN**," tears began to roll down her eyes and all she could do was laugh right along with me.

"See what I'm saying, you flip out on me when things just don't go your way."

"Baby I'm so sorry, it's just I have been working for so many years,"

Chapter 28

Front Page News

Headed down Dale Mabry, "This damn city is so got damn slow!" Julian said while on his way to Carrollwood.

RING RING RING

"What up Pretty Boy?"

"Shit, just chilling on my way to drop some pounds in the suburbs."

"Well, I need you to handle a little business for me. Your mission is to shoot someone in that area."

"Fuck, you know that's my prime area. I don't want to fuck that shit up."

"Are you in or not?"

"Damn"

"Like I said are you in or not"

"Yeah I'm in."

Riding down Dale Mabry to Elrich making a left I began to make my rounds.

5 HOURS PASSED

$30 Grand stashed in the back on my way to pop somebody in the ass.

Who is it going to be . . . . ? Hummmm . . . .

Driving down I seen this Vin Diesel looking mother fucker with a group of white men running down the strip. Yeah he looks like an easy target. Rolling down the window slightly so that they wouldn't get a glimpse of me . . . .

POP

Damn, I caught that mother fucker in the ass. They just told me to shoot someone they didn't say I had to kill someone. Ha haha . . . Let me drop into grandmas and drop this vehicle off. Thonotosassa exit heading to Grandmas with ease. I went to the shed and torched the tag that was on the whip so that no one could link me.

"Big Mommmmmaaaa," I said as I ran through the door. There was no answer.

Must be sleep so I sat back in Grandmas reclining chair with Sunday's left over's and turned on the news.

"Well there was a drive by shooting today. Police say that the victim was a 6'3 black male who was running down the street close to the mall on Gun Highway and everything just happened so fast that they couldn't spot which car it was that sent the bullet out of it. Police are looking for any witnesses or if anyone that knows who could have been involved in this incident to notify them immediately," a news castor stated.

"Kathy wasn't there reports of rising gangs in the Tampa Bay Area.?" Another castor asked.

"Yes, but there is no linkages here, this tragic event happened in broad day light. No one knows who could be a suspect at this point." Kathy said.

"Hell Nawwh, I made prime time news. They won't find me."

"Hey chill, I didn't know you were in here." Grandma said as she walked into the living room with her floral gown.

"Yeah, it's me, Momma, how's it going?"

"Good."

"Now you know you're wrong!"

"Well, I didn't think you were here so I just let loose."

"Huh, what that you said?" as she went to the kitchen.

"Nothing, Momma."

"Well son, don't talk about it, be about it, and get your hips up out of my chair."

"Ahhhh, Momma, you cooking tonight?" I asked as I laid a big one on her cheek.

"Do, I look like Florence from the Jefferson's to you?"

"No, you don't but coming close. You are losing weight?"

"How about I am, they put me on this new medication for my heart and had to change my eating habits."

"I know Aunty Geraldine is all up in your grill making sure you're doing right"

"Yeah she is, told that Meals on Wheels to me send some food. They can cook but I ain't in the capacity where I can't cook for myself."

"I need to call them and tell them to stop sending this food."

"What's the number?"

"I don't know look in the phone book."

"Alright"

"And you know you done messed up. Didn't I always teach you if you go to someone's house and they have things set in a proper way to leave them that way?"

"Yes Mamma."

"Having me miss my Wheel of Fortune."

"Umm Humm, yes I was calling to have you stop delivering meals on wheels to a Miss Lena Thomas located on 1216 Thonotosassa Rd in Thonotosassa, Florida."

Operator, "And you are?"

"Hold as I put her on the phone."

"Momma, telephone."

"Yes suga, this is Lena Thomas, and I'm fully capable to take care of myself. I rather you send your meals to someone who needs it."

"Okay Miss Thomas, I'll go ahead and take care of that for you."

"Thank you."

"Man, Momma you don't even give the lady a chance to say goodbye."

"Well you know business is done. She knows what she needed to do, it's over, time gone."

"What have you been up to today?"

"Nothing much Grandma just handling business."

"How are you going to handle business? You don't even have a steady job. Don't play me for any fool I know what you doing. You better keep your hands clean and lay low. And son, don't do business at your house and don't even try to bring that shit up in here."

"Alright Momma, I have enough respect for you and your house."

Chapter 29

Eye For An Eye

RING RING RING

We have a call for Mr. Lloyd Hawkins from St. Joseph's Hospital? This is an urgent matter to let him know that his brother Reggie is in need of a blood transfusion. Is Mr. Hawkins available?"

"Not at this time but my name is Jaya his fiancé."

"Okay ma'am can you please relay this message. His brother is in critical condition. He is in Intensive Care Unit 402B."

"Oh, not Reggie!"

Running to her cell phone, "Baby, baby your brother has been shot."

"Thank you for calling Lloyd Hawkins unfortunately . . . .

"Damn"

Searching through her cell phone for CVS, "Thanks for calling CVS how may I help you?"

"Yes, May I have the pharmacy?"

"One moment please, as I transfer you over."

"Okay"

"Pharmacy how can I help you?"

"Yes, may I speak to Lloyd Hawkins?"

"Mr. Hawkins is not in today."

"He's not in, okay."

He said he was going to work today. He sure is going to have to come up with a good story for this one. I mean he left the house as if he was headed to work. Let me dial this number again, pacing around the house to clean up just to avoid what was going on. Since he's not answering I'll send him a text message.

Chapter 30

THE SHEET'S ARE PULLED

Arriving at the hospital, Lloyd is greeted by his family and friends.

"How's Reggie?"

"He's okay we need your blood since you guys are a perfect match."

"Alright, no problem. What happened?"

"I don't know if you heard the news, but someone drove by and shot Reggie, they don't know who it is."

Pacing back and forth, "Whoever fucked with my brother is going to get fucked up!"

"Ain't no need for someone else to be harmed," Mrs. Hawkins said as she watched her eldest son in a rage.

"I don't need anything happening to you. You need to calm down." She said.

"Momma, I'm good, it's just in this world how do you expect me to just sit around here and not do something? Whoever did this to Reggie need to be hurt!

"Baby, vengeance is not yours, its God's."

"Yeah, but Momma, this world is mean and some people these days don't' care about me or you."

Giving him that you heard what I said look, "Leave it!"

"Baby, is everything okay, Mrs. Hawkins is Reggie alright?" Erica said with this high pitched voice coming into the waiting room.

"Erica what on earth are you doing here?" Lloyd said as he looked into his mom's eyes.

"Baby, I got the call that Reggie was in trouble. So I rushed right over."

"I'm not your baby, and I told you that we are not together."

30 MINUTES PASS

Erica is still there and in walks Jaya.

"Awwhhh shit," Lloyd said.

"I came over here as soon as I received the call, I tried calling your job and they said you were not there today." Jaya said in a shaking voice.

"Baby, I knew not to call you because I know how you get so stirred up. And I know your nerves is not right," Lloyd said as he approached Jaya.

"Oh no, who is this bitch," Erica rising from the chair.

"Bitch, who the fuck is this Lloyd," Jaya said as her body swayed back and her eyes cutting him like a knife.

With a quick response, "That ain't nobody baby, she's just a friend of the family," Lloyd said knowing he got himself into some shit.

"Your ass wasn't saying that last night," Erica said as she stepped into the direction of Jaya.

"What the fuck I know you ain't tipping around on me with this flaw ass bitch?" Looking at Lloyd, Jaya dropped her Dolce and Gabbana purse and began to start taking off her Dolce and Gabbana earrings. "I don't waste time arguing." Jaya swung and hit Erica right across her face.

Dropping to the floor, Erica tried to regain consciousness. Jaya looked at Lloyd. "You don't even have to say a word because I followed your ass last night to her house."

"Baby, let me explain."

"Shittin me. I'm through. Mrs. Hawkins I didn't mean to come and make a scene. I'll be praying for Reggie. But mother fucker I'm moving my shit out of your house and I'm changing the locks to my house! **IT'S OVER!!!!**

"Hello, Mrs. Hawkins, is everything alright?" LaKesha walks in 2 minutes after Jaya finally got her breath.

"Oh are you seeing her too? Aren't you seeing my brother?"

"Oh nooooo baby I use to be with that, and Reggie's friend. And the looks of it things just don't change . . . Erica could never get enough, stupid hoe." LaKesha said with quickness raising her left hand showing off her diamond ring, "Oh yes, I am seeing your brother!"

The jealousy of seeing another woman with a ring on her hand and not one of her own just added fire to the siring anger that was burning her up on the inside, "Well I tell you, you don't have to ever see this face again Lloyd." Jaya stormed out the door.

"This some fucked up shit, baby don't leave." Sobbing and unable to catch his breath Lloyd just sinks down in the chair.

5 MONTHS HAD PASSED

Someone said that they had seen Jaya come by the hospital. I have not receiving a phone call from her. I just began calling around to everyone I knew. No sign of her. I met up with my Momma and asked her had she heard from Jaya. "Hotep Momma"

"Whatever that supposed to mean son, how are you doing?"

"I'm great. Just came by checking on things. Hotep means peace to you and Ancient Egyptian way of greeting one another."

"Oh that's so nice of you Ray-Ray"

"When was the last time you heard from Jaya?"

"I don't know."

"Did she come by and introduce her new boyfriend to you?"

"Hell no, that girl always has something going. That was the first time I had even seen the guy was at my party. I try telling her things and she doesn't want to listen."

"Well you know what Poppa use to tell me, a hard head always makes what?"

"A hard ass."

"No, the last time I heard from her, she was calling asking me to co-sign for her car. I told her no. She just bought a Lexus Jeep and just lost one of her jobs."

"Well Ma"

"And you know she's not stable. That girl moves every year. She expects me to co-sign for her? I don't know what she's been smoking."

"I don't know why my siblings just totally avoid me?"

"Well if you really want to know, you have both your grandfather's demeanor all over you. The only time they see the real you, is when you're shining.

"But Momma, that don't make any sense."

"Yeah, what don't make dollars don't make sense. Sometimes it's not even all about dollars son. You know that when your Dad died he left you the company, and baby left you more than enough to live for the rest of your life. So your own accomplishments, baby you can stand on your own feet. Your siblings act like someone owes them something. Where did they get that from I do not know. Must be from your Dad's hidden side of family because everyone on my side knows what work ethic is and you know Pop-Pop always had you beside him working at the company.

"Then when Poppa use to get tired of his brother Earl . . . . People that don't hear feel what?"

"Hard. Now boy you are something else. It just amazed me how you can remember so much you were so little. Must have got that from your dad because you know my mind is shot."

"Ha ha ha . . . Momma . . . you remember what you want."

"Humm"

"Well I'll keep calling and see what's really going on." This is very unlike Jayla she always picks up my phone calls when I call or she'll call the very next minute.

The very next week I had spoken with Reid Smith a FBI agent to look in the system to find the where abouts of my little sister and there was no trace. He told me that he placed her cell phone number in a few tracking systems and he couldn't find anything. I showed him a recent picture of Jaya since she was all-star stunted. She cut off her long black hair that Grandma and Momma slaved to keep in a healthy condition, saying she wanted more of a Fantasia look for 2007. My baby girl, where in the world could she be?

Having posted agents at different locations to look around and asking people that Jaya had known. Nothing, I had decided to take a look through Jaya's house. Headed down Nebraska into Avalon, getting through security, I noticed that Jaya's house was remodeled and the girl had a pool on the outside. Now she should know better having some of these folks looking shame in here. But knowing Jaya everyone had to know her, and have visited her house.

Unlocking her door, there was mail scattered all over the floor. I walked in and it was dust everywhere. My heart sunk . . . ohhhh shit. It looked like the house was vacant for quite some time. I picked up the mail off the floor. I placed it on the side table in the living room.

"Jaya are you here?" I yelled hoping to get an answer.

The house was quiet. I walked around the house then went upstairs and still couldn't find her. I went back into her room and looked inside her drawers to see if I could find her. Throwing back the covers trying to see if anything was hidden.

NOTHING

I found a secret chest where Jaya had hidden all of her personal belongings. Pulling back her clothes in her walk in closet, I saw self-taken pictures of her with black eyes and busted lips. Each of them dated and there were notes behind each one of them stating when Lloyd beat her down. I was hurt, my own baby girl keeping this way from me. That mother fucker is going to pay. My eyes began to burn at the anger that I had felt inside. Shit, that Mother Fucker. Bending over to see what was under the bed I saw two letters.

> Baby, please don't leave me. I promise I won't cheat anymore. That bitch didn't mean anything to me. Baby you are the love of my life.
>
> Lloyd

That cheating ass mother fucker. I thought back over the day that I and LaKesha had lunch with Jaya. She did mention that he cheated, but never mentioned anything else especially if that mother fucker beat on her. I would have kicked his mother fucking ass.

> Baby, I said that I was sorry. You won't answer any of my calls. I came by your house and you changed the locks. Yeah, I know I fucked up, but to put my clothes out in front of the house that was really fucked up.
>
> Baby, I said I was sorry.
>
> If I can't have you, no one will have you.
>
> Lloyd

I ran down stairs taken all the evidence that I could take with me and looked through the letters that I had found on the door. I found two more letters.

> I'm coming to the house tonight.
>
> You better be home.
>
> Lloyd

> Yeah I saw your ass out with that mothafucka last night. I have been watching you for the past couple of days. You think this shit is funny huh???
>
> Your family that you so claim you don't have will not know that you're missing.
>
> Watch what I tell you!
>
> Lloyd

RING RING RING UNAVAILABLE NUMBER

"Mr. Jenkins are you up for the reward money? I know who has your sister."

"Who is this?"

"That's none of your concern. I do not want the cops or anyone involved."

"Is this a prank call because you chose the wrong time to play a game? My mother fucking sister is missing. Don't have any fuckin time to be playing around right now."

"Mothafucka who you think you're talking to I said I know where your sister is. If you want her back, you best follow these instructions . . ."

"How the fuck you gone call my phone?"

"That is none of your business. I know the FBI has your phone tapped; I'm going to be calling you back in 5 minutes. You better not give anyone any hints to what is going on."

CLICK

5 minutes passed me by, it seemed like 5 hours . . . sweat just forming out the side of my head. This shit is unreal. Who in their right mind would want to play with someone's life at this point? Gritting my teeth in anticipation everyone had turned their attention towards me so I took the business call in Grandmas secluded office upstairs.

RING RING RING

"Are you alone?"

"Yeah I'm alone. No one knows that I'm talking to you."

"So where am I supposed to meet you."

"Do you have the money?"

"Of course I have the money."

"Mother Fucker you best not forget or your sister will remain missing."

"Okay. I got what you said. What I'm supposed to do."

"Meet a black expedition truck tomorrow at Westshore Mall at 3pm. Don't try to tip no one off, on what's going on or the deal is off. You are going to follow it until the final destination that's where we will do the exchange for your sister."

I arrived to Westshore Mall in my truck. I know I didn't want to be a minute late, so I parked by Sears to make sure that nothing would conflict with the situation. It was beaming hot. People passing by in their normal day to day life while my fucking sister is being held hostage somewhere. Walking around without a care in the world that their life could end at any day and time whether there is another terrorist attack or they just fall dead. Jaya Jenkins would just be another name on a fucking tombstone and no one would fuckin care. Fuck everyone at this point. I want my fucking sister.

Looking at my clock, it was 3pm. This black expedition truck pulls up to the entrance of Maggiano's with black rims and black tints. It was as if this entire event was orchestrated, how in the hell it got through 2pm traffic totally confuses me. I pulled up behind it and flashed my lights and it slowly pulled off towards the exit. Headed down Kennedy Blvd there was so much congestion people tried to come in between me and this vehicle at this point was not happening. All lights were green until we hit North Boulevard and had to make a left turn. College students were everywhere trying to exit the University of Tampa and there were many people in a rush trying to get home from work. Crossing over Cass Street the Expedition signaled to take me into Riverfront Park. Headed back by the pool I knew I had to make sure I had my guns tucked away in some unseen places. I then grabbed the suite case that was filled with 5 million dollars.

A man wearing an all-black suite looking like he was an FBI agent hopped out the truck followed by three other men. "Follow us!"

I walked behind them. There were many people playing tennis and a couple of people playing basketball. Then we walked further down the walkway to a secluded place looking across from the Performing Arts Center. Walking around the corner there was

Jaya was wrapped up, gripped by the arms of Lloyd.

"Mother Fucker is this what it has come down too?"

"Yeah . . . Your little sister left me she doesn't deserve to live at this point."

"Who the fuck are you to decide that. She doesn't owe you shit. I know that there are plenty bitches out there that you can fuck with. The woman that you have in your hands is priceless. I have brought you the reward money. So what's the deal? Are you going to give me my sister or what?"

"Humm, I can respect you enough as being who you are, but she doesn't deserve to live. I know if this was my little sis, I would feel the same way, but you don't understand this bitch lead me on, paying her bills, kissing her ass, she even shamed me in front of my people then, she went on and broke my heart. Man to man, you know that was some fucked up shit, and that shit hurts."

"Like I said breast, her life is not in your hands."

Pulling a gun from his back, "She doesn't deserve to live."

He placed the gun towards Jaya's head; tears began forming at her eyes. She was so scared and afraid. There were scars all over her face.

Keeping my grown man on, I kept a straight face. "I'm willing to let you walk out of here, give me my sister and let all this shit pass. Just let her go man."

A tree limb snapped Crack **POW POW POW . . .**

"I told you not to bring anyone here!" Lloyd screamed.

My posse had followed me. Guns and silencer's shot all of Lloyd's men. Even the ones that were waiting in position behind bushes and trees to shoot were laying dead.

I got close to him. I pulled out my gun. "What's it going to be?"

Tears began falling at his eyes, "Man, I just wanted to prove a point to this bitch that you don't play with a man's emotions. Give me the fucking money and I will disappear."

I threw him the bag. Jaya ran towards me. "Get into that fucking Expedition and get the hell on."

"Fuck her. I have a bitch that's three times finer than her and fuck three times better. I don't need her. Tell your men to back down."

Looking around, "It's alright, situation handled, let him go."

Walking in front of us, to head towards the truck, Lloyd turned back around, "Yeah that bitch you fuckin, me and my brother fucked." He pulled two guns out, "A word out on the street is, that bitch ass brother you got, shot and killed my brother, and his mother fucking days are through, so fuck you mother fucker.

Jaya pulled my gun from my back belt and shot Lloyd right in the chest. Blocking the bullets I was hit in the chest three times as he hit the floor we left.

Chapter 31

Time is of an Essence

Taking off from work today I called Moms since I haven't been to the house in a while.

"You have reached the Jenkins residences please leave your name, number, and the time you called and someone will get back with you as soon as possible."

"Mom, this is Ron calling to see how you were doing. Give me a call when you get this message."

I knew I have been tending to my own life so long that I really don't spend as much time with Moms. She always has been there for me, but I haven't done the same. In life it's just amazing how we spend so much time taking care of things that don't really matter and simply neglect the people that matters the most.

5 DAYS PASSED

It's very unusual not to hear back from Mom. You call her at any time of the day; she will pick up the phone or call you back later on that night.

I was caught up on my work and had decided to leave a little early so that I could stop by and do some grocery shopping at Walmart before I headed home in Davis Island.

I had placed my briefcase in the back. I had opened my car door and reached to get my sunglasses from the adjacent sun visor. Sitting in my Jetta I suddenly felt something moving around in my pocket. Nearly jumping out of my seat and going into a sudden panic. I forgot that I had put my phone on vibrate.

WHHHHHHHHHHHHHHEEEEE . . . God damn nearly peed on myself.

"Hello?"

"Hi sweetie, how are you doing today?" Mom's squeaky voice yelled over the phone.

"I'm fine you nearly scared the BaJesus out of me."

"Did?"

"Yes Ma'am reminded me of that day when I was in Grandma's house when I was younger. That big spider jumped on my back. This time I was able to hold my pee."

"Ha ha ha . . . . Boy you are crazy you must have had too much on your mind?"

"Yes Ma'am I did."

"You know my ears and doors at my house are always open to keep you company."

"Yes Ma'am, but something's I think I have to handle on my own."

"That's it; you need to stop in today. Your phone is free, so I know you're not at work. I have called all your siblings in because I need to talk to each one of you."

"Yes Ma'am"

Getting off from Leroy Selmon Expressway I headed down towards Ybor City through 22nd Avenue to get back on 275 to head north. I have wasted $1.75 and in traffic. I hope she is not going to lecture me today. I should have kept my mouth closed. I know she's going to lecture. Ask me 50 million questions until I break down and tell her everything.

Pulling up to mom's driveway I could see pictures of cats everywhere and just more cats. Huh I don't know how she deals with it.

"Is that you Ray Ray," she said as she came out of the kitchen with a turkey wing wrapped in a piece of paper towel.

"My favorite . . . um um you have started something. I'm not going to sit here and be teased by one turkey leg." Peace . . . I stated as I passed through the living room towards the kitchen. Jaya and Julian had gathered around the big screen to watch

Kissing me with her beautiful red uniform lipstick, Mom hadn't aged much. Just looking at the side of her head you could see this streak of gray in her hair. Her caramel complexion was simply beautiful. She kept her figure in shape by walking three times a week and going out learning how to do the Samba.

"Baby you know the collard greens and the rest of the dinner is not finished," sheewing me out of the way, I stood my position and kept my ground.

"So what do you have up your sleeve?"

"Nothing," she said as she rolled her eyes and embraced my body.

"Um humm, you're hiding something."

"I just felt like cooking today."

Getting Jaya back was a great joy. She would ask every now and then why it took so long to look for her, but thankful that we had rescued her. That mother fucker had her chained in the attic like he was Hannibal.

"I thank you all for coming out to see me today. It has been a long time since we have seen each other. The second thing that I have brought everyone here together is . . . . to let you know that I need the family like none other at this point in my life. I really didn't know how to approach the matter until I talked with my doctors and they let me know that this would be a great time to tell the family. I had been diagnosed with breast cancer two years ago. You didn't see me around because you know I thought I could handle this thing on my own. However they removed the cancer the first time and I was in remission. They told me that I have a chance of living the rest of my life healthy. I had been gone for a few months in and out of chemo. The doctor's couldn't see how things were happening. He says that my cancer came back into a drastic change for the worst," Momma said as she sat back in her chair.

Tears began to form at my eyes. I'm losing the next close thing to my heart. I jumped from the chair to embrace my Mom. Everyone just had tears in their eyes. All getting up to embrace mom, letting her know that we were all there for her. Julian on the other hand could've just stayed home. He didn't even show one sign of remorse. It was as though we didn't even matter at all to him. I don't know what type of shit he's been smoking. He can just get the fuck on with that shit. Momma really doesn't need any of his drama right now in her life.

"Mom I'm always going to be here for you. Whatever you need just give me a call, I know that you have enough to take care of yourself but I will be making more visits to see you."

"Ma," Jaya just sobbed and embraced her, "I'm so sorry to have taken you through so much. I really love and appreciate you for always picking up the phone, even when you knew I was up to no go. I'm sorry. I'm sorry for any problems that I could have caused you. Please forgive me. I'm sorry Ron for taking you through the kidnapping. I'm sorry for it all I'm trying to do better."

Tears just running down her face, "It's okay Jaya, I almost had to take a bat and hit you cross the head to knock some sense in you. I just want you and Julian to get your things together. It really hurts my heart to see you trying to fit in with this new crew of people. You have everything that you need; those people will leave you high and dry when the shit hits the fan."

"I got me Ma. I'll be alright."

"Have you talked to Grandma?"

"No"

RING RING RING

BUZZZZZ BUZZZZ BUZZZZZ

"Whoa still forgot to take it off vibrate."

"Hello," Momma said.

Leaning over the counter with another turkey wing in my hand, I noticed tears started forming at Mom's eyes, "Momma what's wrong?

Lifting her index finger.

Eagerly waiting to see what she had to say. I put the turkey wing down.

"They have taken Grandma to the intensive care unit. A woman ran the red light and swiped Momma's car into another car and she hit a concrete barrier."

"No . . . which hospital is she at?"
"I'll drive."
"Come on I'm driving"
"Let me get my purse and lock the house."
"Okay."

Arriving at St. Joseph's Hospital the emergency room was filled with people. I just thank God for doctors because I know that I can't handle seeing blood. Reaching the intensive care unit all the family was gathered in the waiting room. There were only four people that could be in the room at the time. But no one had entered because the doctors were still in the room observing what was happening to Grandma.

The scene was almost like a family reunion all over again. When they say the dead has arisen. The dead has a risen. There were many people that I hadn't ever in my life seen. Some of them looked like they were walking dead. Must be some of Grandma's friends.

"Hello everyone."

"How's Grandma doing is she alright? The doctors said that she's in a critical state," Aunty Geraldine said.

Tears began to roll down Aunty Louise's eyes. After all those years of fighting with her sisters and my aunts; seeing Aunty Louise cry over Grandma. I just burst out in tears.

"They say that there is a fair chance that Grandma wasn't going to make it. Her Diabetes, high blood pressure, and trauma from the impact are fatal. The only way she would pull out of this is through will power," Aunty Geraldine said.

At this point I just wanted to tell Aunty Geraldine to shut the fuck up but she was the only one talking.

"Baby, it's going to be alright," Momma said as she took a big Kleenex box of tissues out of her purse. "Baby it's going to be all right."

My heart dropped just at the thought of Grandma leaving me . . . . I felt lifeless. Tears just poured down my shirt.

1 hour had passed the doctors were still in searching for answers but could not come back with anything. The doctors came out stated

that Grandma was suffering from brain hemorrhages and she's still fighting for her life. They have stabilized her blood pressure but were not sure.

"We have done all that we could do for your mother. We went in to release the pressure off her brain by removing a blood clot, but at this point there is nothing that we can do for her. I'm sorry that this unfortunate event has occurred at this point. We will allow you to spend the last few minutes so that you can say your last farewells before she passes. There is also the possibility of you donating her organs to another family that needs it."

"Can I see her?" I said tears still rolling down my face.

"Yes I can allow you to see her," the doctor stated.

There were four of us gathered around Grandma. Momma, Aunty Louise, Aunty Geraldine and I. Someone went to find the where abouts of Uncle Al.

"Momma it's your baby. I'm here." Momma stated, "Your Big Girl is here."

"Jean come on out from those woods. You still have to stay with me. You know that Geraldine, Willie Mae, Al, and I can't make it without you. Momma told us to stay together no matter. Please don't leave," said Aunty Louise.

"I'm so sorry for everything I caused." Aunty Geraldine said as she grabbed Grandmas other hand.

Grandma's eyes opened up and she began looking around. It was a peace that came all around her. Tears rolled down her face and into her ears and onto the bed. And this peaceful look came all around her.

I began to get lifted out of my spirit.

There was a glowing light around grandma.

BEEEEEE PR . . . .

Arriving at Momma's house, Julian began pacing back and forth like something scared the shit out of him.

"Momma I have to leave . . . . I got to go. I have to get out of here."

"What's going on Julian?"

"I know you have been protecting me and saving me out of everything but mama I have to do this on my own."

"Baby what's going on? What type of shit you got yourself in?"

"Momma they are looking for me."

"Who is looking for you? Don't matter I have to go. I have to disappear, I love you. This is the last time you will see me."

"Who is looking for you?"

"Don't matter, I have to go. I have to disappear, I love you. This is the last time you will see me."

Tears began to form at her eyes, "Baby you know I have money. I can get you out."

"Momma you can't take care of this one. Kissing her on the cheek he left out the door."

"Baby don't leave!" . . . . crying

Picking up the phone to call Ron—"You have reached the voicemail of Ron Jenkins please leave a message and I'll get back with you as soon as possible.

Sobbing on the phone . . . ."Ron, Julian is gone; give me a call when you get this message."

2 HOURS PASSED

"Momma, what's going on now?"

"Julian said he did something and he has to disappear. Well Momma, you just have to let him go. You can't keep saving him. You have your own life to think about right now."

"Hollering . . . . No Ron, No Ron, that's my child, I'm not going to give up on him."

"Momma, stop it."

"The phone was silent. Momma

"Ohhh . . . . I'm just so worried about that boy."

Sitting back with the family and Lakesha by my side all gathered at Momma's house.

KNOCK KNOCK KNOCK

The crew had come by. That's what I call true friendship.

"Partner you know we had to come see you," Kyle said.

"Thanks man . . . ya'll know"

"Man, we know we had to be here. Grandma was like a Momma to us also and Jaya is like a little sister too your family is our family," La'Gwuan said.

Never seeing a group of men together let alone at an emotional state was something out of the ordinary for LaKesha. Just sitting back in the chaise she went to praying under her breath.

Chapter 32

If it aint one thing it's another

August

A month had passed and I haven't heard anything from this FRAUD guy. I got in contact with the credit bureaus and they're sending me my credit files. They had advised me that it would take 5 to 10 business day before I receive them.

Jennifer and I agreed to meet over at J Alexander's for lunch. I just left College Hill Library and headed toward West Tampa.

I was on my way downtown to my office when my stomach just didn't sit to right. I had decided to take a brief jog around Rowlett Park to get whatever I ate go down. So I took off my Sean-John shit and headed around the corner. Bubble Bubble Bubble . . . oh shit what the fuck. I grabbed my stomach as a little gas rolled around . . . Ummm, may have to take a shit. I just started running a little faster.

Car's where going by. By this time I had made it back towards my truck. Shit I best run a little faster and run for the 7 eleven to let this shit go. Ha ha I walk out leaving a smelly load like I don't know who could have done that.

The sounds of police cars were moving fast in my direction. I heard a helicopter move over my head. Oh shit something must have popped off in the Springs. My tall ass best to get the fuck up out of here before they claim I meet the description of the black man that everyone is looking for. I heard footsteps coming up behind me.

I started running faster. Fear came over me and sweat was just running down my body like a running faucet. There's no way

I'm going down like this. What the fuck am I running for? I was running like a real track star . . . I looked behind me and the cops were chasing me. I ran right through traffic it was everywhere it was 5pm. I headed in the direction of 22nd avenue so that I could hide behind one of those back alleys. I heard police car engines reveling in the back ground . . . sirens were glaring from everywhere. Oh shit. I was met at the corner. They had me cornered right at the gas pump.

"Get down. Get down hand behind you head. Stop running or we'll shoot!"

I looked behind me, oh shit, PD and those crooked ass cops. I just slowed down my pace reaching for my keys I know they are not talking to me.

"**PUT YOUR HANDS UP!**"

I turned around all I know this mother fucker is on me with a Taser gun.

"Ohh shit. What the fuck are you doing? I have my rights. I have done nothing wrong."

"Well you're going to have to use that as your alibi because your black ass is mine. This white cop said. Laughing to his partner. "We got us another one boss"

I just looked at the black man. "Brother I know you're not going to just let him do me like this. He didn't even give me my Miranda Rights before he cuffed me or told me why I was being hand cuffed." *Mr. Matthews, a lawyer friend of mines called it malfeasance of office.*

People walked up to the scene out of nowhere. It was almost like a scene from COPS. Do ya'll see what's happening they didn't even ID me they haven't even followed proper procedures . . . . man these some crooked ass cops.

"You're already in trouble do you really want to go there with this?" a police officer said.

"Watch your mouth son or we are going to charge something else to your list of charges."

I don't believe this shit. I'm sitting in the back of a police car cuffed up. This some shit. DAMN. This ain't even my fault they have false accused me, violated my rights and imprisoned me in the broad day light and everyone sitting around and not doing shit about it. How on earth?

Reaching Orient Road Jail the cops lead me to an empty cell. I called my Momma and told her to get my lawyer down here as soon as possible. I told her what happened and told her to meet me down here.

1 HOUR PASSED

Jennifer was allowed to see me. I had asked where was the lawyer and she had this blank face on her. "So did you get in contact with Charles Haynes?"

"No. I contacted his office and his paralegal stated that he was out on vacation and due to return next week. I didn't know what to do so I called Bryant Scriven.

"He is my father's friend. Yes I know he'll get this taken care of. Shit!!! How in the hell did I get caught up in this shit."

Contact and Visit Us at:

Blue Crown Imperium LLC
www.BlueCrownI.com
BlueCrownImperium@gmail.com